Her Heart's Footprints

A Journey To Love

Poetically
Enigmatic

Library of Congress Cataloging-in-Publication Data is available upon request.

Paperback ISBN 979-8-218-52725-9

ALSO BY POETICALLY ENIGMATIC

POETRY
the day my heart turned... COLD

Her Heart's Footprints
A Journey To Love

Poetically Enigmatic

Her Heart's Footprints

DEDICATED TO EVERY HEARTBEAT AND EVERY NOTE THAT INSPIRES ME TO SPILL MY INK...

Chapters

PREFACE

Over the past few months, I did just what I said I would. That was solely to focus on my work, my family and more importantly, myself. My birthday was just around the corner, and I wanted to do something different this year. I hadn't heard from Zyaire in almost two months. So, I figured that he was now seeing someone else, which was fine. Honestly, I didn't expect him to wait on me to decide who I wanted to have in my life.

I, on the other hand, didn't go out on any dates with anyone else. The only time I ventured out was with some co-workers who I became good friends with. Well, there was that unforgettable time in New Orleans, but I'm not going to think about that either.

Finally off work and as I was shutting down my computer, my phone started ringing. It was Blake's sister, Deadra. Even though, Blake and I weren't together, I still would talk to her from time to time. She is such a sweet, genuine and kind soul.

I answered, "Hi, D! How are you doing?"

"Great! How are you doing?" she replied happily.

"The same. I know your birthday is coming up. Do you have any plans?" She asked this question with no hesitation and seemed quite determined to find out.

"Yes, I plan to go to New York to see Naquita on Wednesday evening and stay until Monday morning."

"Oh ok. Ok. Sounds perfect! I'm sure I'll call you on your birthday but just in case I don't, 'happy birthday'!"

"Thank you so much, D!"

She then said, "I would love to see you sometime soon before the year is up, Sis!"

"Yes ma'am!" Even though Blake and I aren't together, she still refers to me as her sister. Well, to be honest, I do miss seeing and hanging out with her. We said our goodbyes and hung up.

Little did I know that Blake was standing right there with her listening to our conversation. Coincidentally, he had to be in New York this weekend for some interviews. I should have known by Deadra's tone when she asked what my plans were. However, it didn't cross my mind at the time, especially since Blake hasn't tried to contact me in a while. I didn't think anything else of it and started to pack for my trip.

A couple mornings later as I was double checking my bag, I received a text from Blake that seemed out of nowhere. However, if I really thought about it... it kinda wasn't.

The text read, *'Hi Nef. Baby, this is Blake. I wanted to try and reach out to you again to see if you would talk to me. My feelings for you have not changed. If you didn't feel the same for me, I know you would have told me by now. Please talk to me. I love you.'*

My emotions tried to overwhelm me, but I didn't give in to them. He's right. If I didn't love him, I would have already said it. But, of course, I didn't respond to his text. I told myself that I was going to go to New York, see my bestie, have fun and not think about Blake or any other man while I was there.

I arrived at the airport a couple hours early to go through check-in. My flight was supposed to takeoff at 10:45am and land at 6:51pm. It was a nonstop flight; thus, it would be plenty of time to chill and catch up on a few things.

The flight might be time for a chill and relax mode, but I just knew I would be hungry some time or another. There was a convenience store just around the corner. While waiting, I decided to grab a few snacks that I didn't need to hold me until I landed. I usually try not to drink or eat too much while flying because I'm tall and those bathrooms are waaay too small for me.

When it got close to the time to board, I texted my mom and Naquita that I was about to get on the plane. Then I said a prayer before gathering my bag and purse to get in line. Thankfully, the flight went smoothly with only a little bit of turbulence. We arrived later than expected at 7:02pm due to bad weather flying through Colorado. Everyone was definitely ready to get off the plane after that.

As soon as I grabbed my bag and exited the plane, I rushed out to see if there were any cab drivers available. Luckily, I was able to get a young lady that was very nice and helpful. She was telling me about some cool places to go to for food and just to have a good time. One of those places she told me about was a poetry spot since she had recognized me from social media. That was a trip because I don't get on it very much. She said that a couple of the poetry spots that she follows in Las Vegas and L.A. have some video of me performing. I was shocked, of course. It was a good thing that I had a book of poetry with me. I signed it and gave it to her as an early Christmas present. She was ecstatic!

The drive from the airport to the hotel was over 40 minutes long. So, by the time I made it to the hotel it was around 8:30pm. I gave the young lady a tip and thanked her for her hospitality. I was so tired even though I had slept a few hours on the plane.

Check-in to the hotel was quick and painless. My room was on the sixth floor at the end of the hallway. I walked into the room and that was basically all I remembered the next morning as I woke up. My clothes were still on like I had just left my house in Vegas to go to the airport.

A moment after opening my eyes, my phone rings. It was Naquita yelling excitedly telling me to get up. I was definitely awake now after hearing all of that in my ear. I went down to the lobby to get her so that she could come up to my room while I got dressed. We yell (hotel yell) when we saw each other and hugged.

"I'm so happy to see you, girl!"

"I knooooow. It's only been a few months, but it still seems like forever. We have to stop that and see each other more often."

"Yes, we do! Let me put on some clothes and then we can grab some breakfast."

"So, uh, have you heard from Blake?" Naquita wasted no time in asking about him.

"He actually texted me yesterday morning. I'll show you when I get out of the shower." When we got back to the room, I ran to get in the shower. Naquita went to look out of the window at the view. When I came out of the bathroom, I grabbed my phone to show her the text from Blake.

"Girl, forgive this man and be happy. You know you love him and want to be with him. Ya'll have been apart long enough."

"I-I just don't want to be hurt again. I can't. I just can't."

"Honestly, Nef, I don't think he meant to hurt you. I really don't. Blake seemed to love her at one point, yes... but he just wanted to make sure that no crumbs were left from what you've told me; plus, she lied to him not too long after that. So,"

"Yeah... Let's change the subject," I say while rolling my eyes. "Where are we going to eat?"

We decided on a place around the corner from the hotel, very popular from what the driver told me last night. Naquita gathered our purses as we headed towards the elevator just cackling away.

Coming out in the lobby, I see a silhouette that looked very familiar.

He turned around and I saw his face. It was Blake. "Oh... my... God?!" I said as I stopped walking. I was frozen.

"Girl, what?! What is it?"

"Blake. Blake is over there." (I whispered.)

"Where?!"

"Ohhhhhhh, shit! Damn! The pictures still don't do him justice! Go over there and talk to him." Blake had gotten a fresh cut and shave and had on a black suit with a white lower cut shirt underneath.

"No, I will not!"

"Well, it looks like you don't have to anyway, because he's coming over here. Yesssss!" (Naquita said teasingly.)

I tried to move to go the other way, but Naquita blocked me. "Girl!"

Here he comes flashing that hypnotizing smile with a side of dimples as his eyes sparkled with every step. We haven't seen each other in a few months, that is, not since New Orleans. The butterflies gathered immediately when I realized it was him. I got so nervous. At that moment I felt my blood begin to rush to every part of me as if I was feeling the steam from a hot shower. I definitely missed him.

TRAUMA

I grew up in a small town when life was much simpler. We played in the water of the fire hydrant during summer months; used our hands as rackets to play tennis; and used a crack at the end of the parking spaces or the sidewalk as the net to play volleyball. Let's not forget that you had to be in the house when the streetlights came on or else.

There were mobile phones as big as the headsets of house phones. TVs that looked like huge boxes taking up almost the whole wall of the living room. As a child, you were the antenna and the remote control. I definitely can't forget about huddling in front of the wall heater that warmed up the living room at grandma's house. If I wasn't over there or my great aunt's, I would walk around the apartment complex with a boombox hoping someone would challenge me to a dance. Plus, I always had a bag of white cheese popcorn. Don't ask. I have no idea, except it was so good.

As you can see, there are some things I do remember but some that I don't. A lot of the memories are only what I've been told, and I guess my mind formed a forever image. I often wonder if it's because there was something that happened to me; or maybe it was something that I was blocking so that I wouldn't remember. I'm really not sure.

However, there are a few other things I do recall like being the only girl on the basketball court most days. I must admit that I was a tomboy. I always got along better with boys than girls and it is still true now.

The basketball court where everyone would play was literally around the corner. So, that lets you know that I didn't have a choice, to say the least. Basketball was my first love; and in case you're wondering, 'Yes,' I still have that shooter's touch.

My first job was at 16 working for a local restaurant. My town was quaint and cozy, so much so, that I could ride my bike to work from where I lived. It was truly convenient, and I stayed there for the rest of high school. During the summer months while I was in

college, I would come home and work, as
well.

     For me, growing up was truly not
for the weak. I was constantly bullied
for my dark complexion. Plus, being
without a father made me question
everything about me. I always wondered
what was wrong with me for him to not
love me enough to want to be in my life
but love the other children that he had
and be in their lives.

     With these feelings and the
constant name-calling, my self-esteem
was very low throughout the years
because of it. I felt like I was not
meant to be loved; thus, I developed a
hard interior; yet, soft exterior that
was easily crumbled. Because of this,
it took me a long time to love myself
and realize that I was enough just the
way I was. If I knew then what I know
now, I would have told them to kiss my
ass.

     As I mentioned, I loved
basketball, but there was one other
thing that kept me going, WRITING. It
was my therapy without actually going
to a therapist. It was how I coped with
any and everything that was going on in

my life no matter what the situation
was. So, I either had a basketball or
pen and paper in my hand... sometimes
even both.

        Writing was and still is my other
first love. The feeling of seeing
someone react the way you hoped they
would will never get old.

        Reciting poetry is about the only
place where I feel most comfortable
(other than a basketball court). There
is no shyness. My natural self is
'showcased' when in front of a crowd
doing poetry. It is an absolute
heavenly feeling that is beyond
peaceful and serene... an outer body
experience that I have and will always
welcome.

        College was an interesting part of
my life. Since I didn't play
basketball, I kept my head in the books
and, of course, with an extra pen and
paper. There were several poetry events
where I would perform. As I said
earlier, to see the reactions from the
audience will always be a feeling like
no other. I definitely can't forget
about the frat and sorority parties.

They were certainly off the chain, and I loved every minute of them. I'm smiling now as I reminisce.

Being shy, I didn't have a boyfriend during college. However, there was one guy that I had a *major* crush on. His name was Zyaire, but I wasn't the only one. All of the girls did. I didn't think he noticed me like that, but he was always nice to me. He was probably too distracted by all of the other girls to see it. I certainly didn't try to make it obvious, at least that's what I believed.

There were a few ladies that I hung out with all throughout my college days; thus, this is when I met my best friend Naquita. We had mutual friends and were introduced to each other one random day. I bet you think she and I hit it off at first, because she's now my best friend. However, no; that's not exactly how it went.

At first, I actually believed that she didn't care too much for me, but I was mistaken. Ever since then, we have been besties. One thing that I have always loved about her is that she never changed. She was and always has been the same Naquita. She always spoke her mind whether you wanted to hear it or not. I like to call her the voice of reason. Naquita is my sister from another mother, and I will always be grateful for having her in my life.

To be honest, I guess you could really say that I bloomed at a late age. So, that means that I was a virgin until I was 25. He was a mistake that I still wish I could take back if I could. He was **the** worst person that you could ever imagine... a manipulative, conniving, lying, abusive poor excuse of a human being. No one should ever refer to him as a **man**. He was methodical in *every* evil scheme he could think of to ruin me in *any* way possible.

His name was Shawn... a straight character, to say the least. He truly should have been an actor because of the way he had me believing and hanging on every word he said. Shawn told me he loved me first. Of course, it was all a part of his twisted game... telling my friends and my family how much he cared. I was HIS, but he was NOT mine.

I was young and naïve, and he was my first. My heart no longer belonged to me anymore. He held it tightly in his hands, so much so, that it would only beat with his command.

I was traumatized by him. He broke me in more ways than I wanted to admit. If you looked up bullshit in the dictionary, you would have seen Shawn's picture with an arrow pointing right at him. In that same pic, he would have been smiling because he had no conscious whatsoever. Shawn didn't care who he hurt as long as he got what he wanted.

During this whole *situationship* that lasted for over a year, Writing was definitely my escape... from myself... from him... even if it was for just a moment. I welcomed every letter... every word that I wrote like this one called 'HE STOLE':

I feel my heartbeat
Weakening
With every poke
My soul being pulled
Deepening
With every jolt

I feel myself falling
Strengthening
Your aura
As your smile widens
Causing more horror
in
My life
Flashing
Before my eyes
Deeply saddened by the visions
I cry
My teardrops forming
Huge puddles
Resembling quicksand
That surrounded me
As I stretch out my hand
But no one sees me
So, no one
Grabs it
As I scream
But my voice
No one hears
As I slowly continue to sink
Panting heavier
More tears
I lose sight of all reality
As the flood of reluctance
Of uncertainty
Enters my nose

I close my eyes
My breath
So faint
Not being able to fight anymore
I just lie and wait
Because
He
Stole

I remember one day that I was over his house *(what I thought was his house)*. He had always told me that he had a 'female roommate,' but I had never met her... officially. Apparently, a neighbor called her and told her that another woman was at her house. Shawn and I were sitting in the living room talking when we heard tires screeching up the street into the driveway. He looked out of the window and sees her rush out of the car running towards the door.

Whispering, he said, "Baby, you gotta go!"
"Why, Shawn?!" I asked.
"I'll explain later!"
"What?! Why?!" I asked him again.

She then rushed in yelling at him. While she was doing that, I slid out the door running to my car. I quickly got in and drove off. This was certainly the beginning of the end for us. Although, it should have been the end at that very moment but really before that.

Later I found out that she kicked him out of the house. Of course, he lied to me saying that they just couldn't get along. Shawn said that she was jealous of him being with someone else. He told me that she wanted to be with him, not the other way around. So, he had to get an apartment.

A little before that day, he had started getting more aggressive with me. The first time that he put his hands on me, I stayed with him even though deep down I knew better. I was convinced that it was an *accident* because that is what he said it was... that he would never push me like that again. Of course, I was so wrong. I was "in love" so I thought.

On one occasion that I so clearly remember, Shawn and I had an argument.

I left his place not wanting to go home, because I was scared to stay at my apartment. Naquita was there for me as she always had been. She was in her last year of college, and I had already graduated.

I called her in the middle of the night asking if I could stay there until the next morning. When I got to her dorm, Naquita didn't ask any other questions but knew that I needed help. She allowed me to stay. Luckily, she didn't have a roommate; so, I was able to sleep in the bed on the other side of the room.

The next and last time Shawn and I got into it. I had bruises all over my body when I woke up the following day. The sun was shining brightly through the window, but he was still asleep. The devil only sees darkness and doesn't recognize light.

I had stayed at his place, and he had been drinking heavily. He was mad about how his week had gone and started arguing with me out of nowhere. Then Shawn put his hands on me, releasing all of his frustrations out on me. I tried to fight him off, but he was 6'5" and 250 lbs. Even though I was 5'9" and 160, I sill tried. After we fought, he passed out due to being sloppy drunk. Since I was in such pain from the chaos, I cried myself to sleep next to him.

When I woke up the next morning, I gathered my things and slowly walked out of the bedroom towards the front door. Luckily, it didn't creak when I opened it, so I was able to walk out and close the door quietly.

I called my mom on the way home to tell her what had happened. She was very upset because she didn't know anything about what I was going through. I hid it very well. It was hard for me to talk to her about it, but I did finally.

As soon as I told her, she drove down to make sure that I was safe and stayed with me for a few days. Shawn did call and text me, but I didn't answer or respond. So, he came over banging on the door like he owned the place.

"Is that him?" My mom asked angrily.

    I looked out of the peephole to
see if it was. I whispered, "Yes, it's
him."
    Mom swung the door open and that
was all she had to do. Shawn didn't try
to do or say anything else when he saw
her standing there. For some reason, he
was literally scared of her, and I was
thankful that he was. Well, I won't
lie. My mom does have a stare that
would scare anyone straight. The next
day, I had a restraining order put on
him. Shawn didn't bother me again.
    About seven years later, I saw him
in a grocery store. We just so happened
to walk up on each other. All the
terrible memories came rushing back as
he was trying to talk to me. I don't
even know what he said, because I got
away from him as fast as I could. Not
trying to make a scene, I hastily
walked out of the store and sped home
crying. It took me a moment to calm
down. What helped was writing the
following poem called 'You're Deaf
Now'...

can't you feel it
my love growing older and colder everyday

you must hear it
the sound of my love slowly tick
tock
ticking away
those feelings that rained down upon me
will soon completely evaporate
and escape
from this jail cell
this man-made hell
that you put me in
what?!
you can't tell
by the way that i look at you with
spiteful eyes
or the way i sigh
when i see you
wondering why i cared for you
my heart - trapped by you
my love - abused by you
you
are the epitome of a liar
told me i was like a highly valued painting
and that you were the only buyer
boy please
you didn't buy shit
you are nothing but a thief
who stole my heart
and blindly robbed me

of my innocence
carved me into an ice statue that if touched
i'd break
so to love again, i can definitely wait
since loving you was definitely a mistake
and guess what
every time you thought i melted because of the wrath of
you
i faked it
yep, every time
formed the image of another man in my mind
to pass the time
away
as my love grew older and colder everyday
soon
another man will be taking your place
and now the sound of my love slowly tick
tock
ticking away
has burst your eardrum...

A moment after I finished writing,
I realized that this part of my life
was finally over. I was not going to
let him destroy what I had worked so
hard on. 'Til this day, I don't know

where Shawn is and could really care less. I'm just hoping that no one else fell victim to his lies and schemes.

For a while after this, I just focused on myself and healing; trying to be the best that I could be for me and for me only. It is still a work in progress; I'm never satisfied. I continue to strive for excellence within myself. It is true what they say. You can't love someone else without loving yourself first. Self-care is an ongoing process that you must continue to practice daily.

LONG OVERDUE

About six months ago, I moved to Vegas... by myself. My previous relationship had become what seemed like a routine day in and day out. There was no spontaneity, no date nights, no walk-by butt slaps, nothing. The fizzle had fizzed out and neither of us were happy but didn't fully want to admit it. Our love was still there, but we outgrew each other in more ways than one.

He and I seemed to want different things at this point in our lives. I wanted stability and adventure and he just wanted to make ends meet and chill at home. So, we pretty much slowly accepted the fact that our time together was over, even though it was hard to let go. Now, don't get me wrong. We had some great times, but we also had some bad ones; the bad just seemed to outweigh the good. Dalvin and I had been together for six years but never married.

Also, coming from a small town, his mom moved with him and his two brothers when they were young after her divorce. Dalvin was an honor roll student from the very beginning and ended up going to the same college as I did. Since he was a few years older, he graduated a year before I started. He was a marketing genius, but his true passion was art.

I bet you are wondering how we met. Well...

It was a Wednesday afternoon in the middle of June. The temperature was around 87 degrees with surprisingly low humidity for that time of year. I was sitting in the food court at the mall eating bourbon chicken, fried rice, steamed cabbage and carrots, vegetable egg roll plus sweet tea in one of those plastic cups. The plates were always packed to the brim. So, I was definitely going to have leftovers for later.

I saw him from a distance staring at me. He was at the same spot getting a plate. When we made direct eye contact, I quickly looked away hoping he didn't see me looking at him. A few minutes later, I felt someone walk up to my table. When I looked up, it was him.

"Hi. Excuse me. My name is Dalvin. Are you expecting anyone to come and sit here with you?"

"Hi Dalvin. No, I am not."

"I saw you from across the way and was in awe to be honest. So, I had to come over here to see if I could get to know you. Do you mind if I sit down with you?" Dalvin asked as he put his hand on the back of the chair. He didn't try to wow me with pickup lines... just plain old conversation and that had me intrigued.

Dalvin's complexion was sun-kissed caramel. He had a low faded haircut with a goatee. His eyes were hazel and angled. He was simply just handsome. I said to myself, 'No, I am the one who is mesmerized.' He was dressed in sportswear from head to toe; not sagging which was a definite plus.

As he sat down, Dalvin said, "I didn't catch your name. What is it?"

"Nefertiti." I said innocently.

Dalvin said, "That fits you perfectly." That made me blush and I smiled as I took another bite. "Do you live around here?"

Still smiling, I answered, "Yes, I do. I'm actually here on my lunch break. What about you?"

"I stay downtown by the river... just out here enjoying this beautiful weather. I am off this week and decided to do a little shopping for this upcoming birthday bash next weekend that they have been advertising about on the radio."

"Oh yeah, I heard about that."

"Are you going by chance?" asked Dalvin.

"No, I thought about it but stopped at that."

"How about we go together?" Dalvin asked as he began eating.

"I don't know you like that. If we were to go together, I would meet you there."

"That's fine with me. If you had said anything other than that, I probably would have ended the conversation right then," Dalvin said smoothly.

We both laughed. "So, we have a little over a week to get to know more about each other before then."

"That is true," I said with an agreeing look of longing to know more about this man sitting in front of me.

Over the next few days, we continued to talk on the phone and text. The night conversations were so long that sometimes we ended up going to sleep on each other. We'd laugh at the other when realizing what happened.

The weekend that we met I had to go out of town for a business trip. Those days passed by so fast that I really didn't feel like I went anywhere.

When I returned home that following Monday afternoon, I saw that I had a voicemail. After placing my bags down, I listened to it and was in shock. It was the apartment management saying that I had a delivery in the office.

I wasn't expecting anything and was beyond curious as to what it could be and who it was from. So, I hurried off to the office not caring about changing my clothes first.

The apartment manager smiled as I walked in, "Hello Nefertiti. How may I help you?"

"Hi, I received a voicemail stating that I have a delivery that was here in the office." I said with an eager tone.

She responded with, "Oh yes! One moment."

It was a bouquet of red roses and a teddy bear. The note read, 'I hope you had a wonderful, safe trip! See you soon... Dalvin.' I was floored because no one had ever sent me flowers before. Oh, he was laying it on thick and I welcomed it.

When I came back home, I placed the flowers in the sun to make sure they stayed beautiful as long as possible. They were already in a vase with water. Then I sat on the couch holding my bear and called Dalvin. "Hi, there. Thank you for the flowers and bear. They are beautiful."

"Just like you... I'm glad you like them."

Our 'courtship' continued from there. We became great friends before anything else. Dalvin knew that there had only been one man before him; so, he didn't pressure me. After about 4 months, we finally had sex and it didn't stop for a while. We moved in together after a year and a half of dating.

Everything was wonderful at first but then something happened, and WE just didn't work anymore. I didn't want to believe it, but it was true. I loved Dalvin more than anything but not more than myself. I could feel that I was losing me again.

I realized that I wanted more.

More importantly, I needed more.

Dalvin and I did talk about marriage in the beginning of our relationship. He told me that he had been married once before and wasn't sure if he wanted to do it again. I understood that and was indifferent about it. If it happened, it happened. If it didn't, it didn't.

Those types of conversations ceased pretty early in our relationship. We basically stopped being 'together' and just lived together, almost like roommates. It wasn't that I wanted to be with anyone else. It was just that I felt he settled, lost the drive that I had

fallen in love with. Dalvin was content
with our situation, but I wasn't. I
put him above everything else including
myself. I was losing who I was in more
ways than one. *Everything was about
him, not us.*

     As I mentioned, every day seemed
like a struggle just being together. *I*
was lonely even when he was right
there. Smiles, laughs, gentle kisses
and caresses were few and far between,
if any. The distance between us kept
getting longer. New walls were built.
Previously fallen walls were rebuilt
even taller. It was hard to even look
each other in the eye most of the time.
My heart no longer yearned for him like
it used to whenever I saw him or heard
his voice. The coldness in me that I
had put away years ago began to
resurface and there was nothing that I
could do to stop it, except leave.

     So, I started looking for jobs out
of state... Texas... California...
Arizona and Nevada specifically Las
Vegas. The first time Dalvin and I went
to Vegas, I fell in love with it. The
atmosphere was contagious, and I
developed an itch from it that stayed

with me after leaving. I am not a gambler; so, it wasn't that. It was just something about the air there that had my nose wide open. It smelled and felt like HOME away from home.

Dalvin could tell there was a shift in my feelings towards him. I wanted to make it work but things were not right between us. My days and nights started to feel longer and longer. Deep down I knew what needed to happen. I had to go. In realizing this, I wrote the following poem called, "I DO NOT."

Sounds so routine
A ploy to keep me green
Empty syllables
No real meaning
Just empty promises
You think it keeps my heart dangling on a leash
But only fuels my hate
My anger
My disappointment
In you
For you
I no longer lust
Nor do I yearn

For you
To
Do what you do
Actually
I despise you
The little things that used to give me a rush
The subtle touches that would make me blush
Now only gives me utter disgust
You
Did this to us
Never will I look at you the same way
I have to pretend to go along with these childish games
you play
It's getting harder and harder to keep my sanity everyday
Constantly praying for the opportunity
That I can leave
Be whole
Feel alive
Be free
Be me
Never will I want to change my name again

About two months after I started applying, I got offered my dream job in Vegas working for a professional sports team as a Data Consultant with a six figure salary. I was super excited and sad at the same time because I needed to tell Dalvin. He was still at work when I found out about this. So, I texted him to let him know that we needed to talk when I got home.

I arrived a few minutes before him and was sitting on the couch. He walked in and saw my head down. "Baby, what's wrong?"

"I - I received a call saying that I got the job in Vegas that I told you about."

With disappointment in his voice, he said, "What?! You did?!"

"Yes."

"Are you... are you going to take it, Nef?!"

"Yes, I believe I am, Dalvin. It's... it's my dream job and in my dream city. You know that."

Dalvin's voice was trembling as he spoke. "So, you are really going to leave me, huh? You really about to fucking leave?!"

"Dalvin, you can come with me. We can start all over. We-"

He interrupted me. "I told you I wouldn't go. So, I'm not going."

In a hurt tone, I asked, "You're not?!"

"No, I'm not," he yelled.

"Obviously, you have made up your mind about us and it... it doesn't look like you are going to change it, either... or was never going to," I said sadly.

"No, I'm not going to change my mind. The fact that you started looking in the first place told me how you really felt... and Nef."

I started crying and he was tearing up.

"Nef, I'm tired... tired of going back and forth with you... about us... about the same things. I love you. I really do but it seems as though we just aren't meant to be."

We started sobbing, realizing that this was really the end of us. It will be a new beginning for me and a new beginning for him... just not together. I'm hoping that this will push him to finally start the art business that he had always wanted to do.

Dalvin is an incredibly talented and intelligent man. I felt like he was letting it all go to waste, but apparently, he didn't feel the same. It was like he didn't want it enough nor did he want US enough.

LETTING GO

For the next month, we slept in separate rooms. The mornings were spent dodging each other, barely speaking or acknowledging the other's existence. Each night was cold and lonely up until the last one.

That day I had to do some last minute errands and visits to friends and family. The drive back to the house seemed like one of the longest rides I had ever had. I backed into the driveway in my rental as I had already shipped my car and other belongings to Vegas. For a moment, I sat there taking in the realization that this was the last day that I would be here. I picked up my purse and turned off the car slowly getting out of it.

As I walked up to the door, the aroma of food filled my nose. When I walked in, I was surprised to see Dalvin cooking. "Hi Dalvin," I said reluctantly but still trying to sound happier than I was.

"Hi. I-I am making your favorites... grilled chicken, baked sweet potato and broccoli."

"Oh, wow! Thank you for cooking."

"You're welcome. I didn't want our last night to be so awkward. I still love you and I always will. I wanted us to leave each other on a good note. You know."

"Yes, I know. I wanted that, too, Dalvin."

"We were always good friends before anything."

"That's true." I said as I took my purse to the bedroom and kicked off my shoes. I stood there for a couple of minutes fully realizing that this was the last night that I would spend there. Then I went back downstairs to the kitchen.

"Have a seat. It's almost ready."

"Ok," I said as I washed my hands and sat down at the table.

I just kept staring... watching him pay attention to every detail of plating the food. Dalvin put our plates on the table and poured some tea for us. He sat down and we said grace for the last time together. Then we began eating. The meal was excellent. Dalvin could throw down in the kitchen when he wanted to. We didn't say much during dinner but mainly looked at each other knowing that our season was coming to an end.

After dinner, we cleaned up the kitchen together, as we so often would do before our current situation. It was getting late. So, I told Dalvin that I was going to take a shower due to my early morning flight. He nodded.

When I first got in the shower, I stood there for a moment with my eyes closed just letting the warm water run all over me. Then suddenly, I heard the door open; it was Dalvin.

"Uhm, can I join you?"

"Yes," I said as I opened my eyes seeing him get in the shower with me.

He let the water run all over him for a few seconds as we looked at each other. Then we started to kiss. He picked me up leaning me against the shower wall. We made love in the shower for the first and last time. Afterwards, Dalvin let me back down as we gazed at each other for a moment. 'Where was this before?!' I said to myself. He didn't say a word, but I saw his eyes start to tear up as if he was about to cry. Both of us quickly looked away and continued to take our showers.

No other words were said between us the rest of the night. This time, we slept in the same bed. He pulled me close to him hugging and holding onto me as if to say goodbye.

About two and a half hours later, I woke up because I had to use the bathroom. When I came back, I couldn't go back to sleep. So, I pulled out my pen and paper from my bag. That always helped me to relax and clear my head. Then I sat in the chair next to the bed and looked over at Dalvin. I had an immediate feeling of inspiration and wrote the following poem called "IT'S YOUR LOSS":

I was so excited
So impassioned
Because my heart only belonged to you
But now that it's over
I don't know what I am gonna do
Because I mean
I was mesmerized
Floating on cloud nine
Because the idea made me so blind
Thinking that one day you'd be all mine
It was distorting
Contorting

My reality
Causing my fallacies
To seem so real
Because of the way you would make me feel
When…
But still…
I was sitting around
Reliving over and over
The sights and sounds
Of
You
The way you so
Skillfully moved
Made me desire to feel every part of you
In so many ways
My heart
My mind
My body
My soul
Forever and always
I wanted to be the one to brighten your days
To be your backbone
Your clutch
To lift you up
Whenever times got rough
I would get so elated
By your presence
So enraptured

So enchanted
By your aura
Your essence
Seemed to be the one to alleviate all of those past
heartaches
That are still causing these present day headaches
But I guess I made a mistake
So, uh…
You can definitely forget about that figure eight
Since…
Now that I'm overly excited and impassioned
Because my heart no longer belongs to you
So happy that it's over
It's your loss, Boo….

The next morning, Dalvin was kind enough to accompany me to the airport. My flight was supposed to leave at 8:00am. However, we left a little earlier because I had to drop off the rental car. The whole ride was quiet with occasional stares with puppy dog eyes that said more than words could ever express.

A friend of his followed us there to pick him up once we said our goodbyes. After returning the rental, he helped me with my bag and walked me into the airport area towards check-in. Our last embrace lasted for a couple minutes. We didn't want to let each other go, but it was time. He then kissed me on the forehead. We said our goodbyes and I walked to the check-in area. It seemed like I could feel Dalvin staring at me while I was walking away. I didn't look back at him because I think I would have stayed if I did. *Good-bye Dalvin.*

Check-in was a breeze. The lines weren't too long, just yet. Going through the metal detectors was even less hassle. I found my terminal and sat there for about an hour listening to music. While waiting on my flight, I was sad, yet happy at the same time. My new life was waiting on me and it was only a few hours away. My old life was like an old picture that you look at with a reminiscing smile, then sit it back on the dresser or living room table to always remember but keep it at arm's reach.

The airplane pulled up at the terminal and the previous passengers exited. Some sleepy. Some sad. Some crying as they were about to see their family or friends. Some were even mad as they were about to miss their next flight. It was a whole mixture of emotions.

While looking at everyone's expressions, I then heard the boarding agent say that it was time to get lined up to get on the plane. My seat was closer up front; thus, my wait in line was not that long.

I boarded the plane, placed my bag in the overhead bin and then buckled my seatbelt. I sat there with my eyes closed trying not to be overcome with emotion. Then almost immediately, my breathing and body relaxed as I opened my eyes. About fifteen minutes later, we took off. I had a window seat and looked out until I couldn't see the city any longer... just clouds and blue skies. It was a bittersweet moment.

Thankfully, my flight was nonstop. So, I was able to take a nap, but I couldn't sleep most of the time. I was overjoyed as my thoughts were consumed with starting this new chapter. When I was awake, I listened to music, watched a few TV shows that I had previously downloaded and wrote a few verses.

When we landed, I picked up my rental because my car hadn't arrived at my place, yet. I had just shipped it two days ago. So, it was supposed to be there tomorrow afternoon. My apartment was only 15 minutes away from the airport which was ideal. Driving down the street from the airport was such an enlightening moment. I went straight to pick up my keys from the leasing office. The people there seemed genuinely nice and concerned. They gave me additional pamphlets of the city and took the time to answer any and all of my questions.

The complex was small, charming and gated not too far from a park. So, there were a lot of huge trees that made the scenery feel more like home than I thought it would.

That drive to my place felt so long even though it was only 2 minutes away. It was a townhouse that came available at the last minute, just for me it seemed. My new place was modern and cozy with two bedrooms, two and a half baths plus a study.

I walked in going through the small hallway leading to the living room and placed my bag down. I sat on the floor for a few minutes taking in the fresh air. I was... HOME. So, I decided to take out my pen and paper to write a little something called 'Fresh Air'.

I inhale
and
a cloud of trapped jumbled alphabet
forming a three-page letter is exhaled
floating across the room
causing a mild stench
to be inhaled
wrinkling his nose
absorbed by his grey matter
an eyebrow is raised
as if to say
*"What the f***"*
and an empty cloud is exhaled
I get choked up
by the gust of wind from the open windows
forcibly pushing the air up my nose
causing me to abruptly awake
as a huge tear slowly rolls down my face
I sit up

trying to regain consciousness
blinking to raise my heavy eyelids
to
a room filled with emptiness
no rolls of thunder bouncing off my eardrums
no muffled laughter on the right side of me
no creaking noises slowly becoming faint into the other
room
no more outside layers thrown all around
no more empty purses due to constant handouts
no more fallacies trying to hide behind those three words
so i clinch the sheets closer to my mouth and scream
"Freedom"
then exhale
inhale repeatedly
breathing fresh, serene air

When I finished writing, I stayed in that same spot in complete silence. I wanted to just be in the moment; plus, I loved the feeling that I had. After about 30 minutes, I decided to go to the store to pick up a few items... air mattress, towels, skillet and pot plus toiletries amongst other things. My job doesn't start for another week and a half which meant that I had some

time to 'try' to unwind and tidy up a
bit.

       I was so excited about my new
position. For the first couple of weeks
or maybe a month, I'll have to be in
the office most of the time.
Afterwards, I'll be working from home
only going in for required meetings or
emergencies. Nothing about the
schedule was completely concrete, but
it didn't matter, because I felt this
opportunity was what I had been waiting
on. I was ready for it.

       This was my first night without
Dalvin for what seemed like forever. It
was probably one of the longest nights
I had ever had. I cried most of the
night because I missed him. I also
cried because this was the first time
in a while that I had felt that rush of
inspiration pierce through my veins. It
was a new sense of self-discovery and a
journey that I had longed for. I needed
this more than I thought. I was
genuinely happy for once in my life and
welcomed what was to come.

       Over the next few days, I was able
to find a nice chocolate sectional with
a chaise that I had always wanted plus

a 5 piece black dining room set. The chairs had chocolate cushions to match the sectional which was absolutely perfect.

Although things seemed like they were coming along, I did feel lonely without Dalvin. I mean how could I not. We were together for quite a while. I really believe that we just got way too comfortable with each other. The excitement of being together was no longer there for either of us.

A couple times during the next few days, I almost called him, but I stopped myself. There was nothing left to say. What's done was done and it was for the best. To have loved someone that deeply for so long just doesn't go away overnight, if ever.

THE ONE

I know you probably want to know more about Blake, THE - Blake - Lovingly. He is the one who makes everyone pause when he is present... the one who makes 32 degrees feel like 212... the one who makes my heart beat to the rhythm in his walk. So, here you go.

Blake was born in Seattle on February 25th. He and his family moved to New York when he was one. As a child he was a little mischievous but what kid wasn't. His dad, Antthony, was a lawyer and was very strict with him and his sister.

His mom, Grace, like mine, was a teacher who taught for about 15 years. However, cooking was always her first love. So, she decided to start her own catering business and retire from teaching. Blake was in the kitchen helping her from the very moment he could see over the counter taking in all the tricks of the trade. He told me that it was and still is some of his favorite moments with her. Whenever he's home, he makes sure that he has that kitchen time with his mom no matter what.

Of course, you know this means that Blake is a 'foodie.' He always told me that if he wasn't acting then he would be a chef. Having had a quite a few dinners from him, I certainly believe that he would have given any one of them a run for his or her money if he solely focused on it. The drive and determination that he has makes me whole heartedly believe that.

Blake's mindset is one of the first things that really attracted me to him. Well, let me rephrase that and be perfectly honest, he is DEFINITELY easy on the eyes. He is every bit of 6'3' with a sun-kissed caramel complexion. *I know what you are saying, 'Nef, you really like those sun-kissed caramel men, huh.' It really doesn't matter. He and Dalvin just happened to be the same complexion.*

But anyway, back to Blake. He normally wears a goatee but sometimes grows out his full beard especially during the winter months when he's not working. He has a gaze that will snatch your soul within a second. His eyes have never lied to me, not that he ever has. Not to mention, his body... whew!

He stays in shape, but his weight fluctuates depending on whatever the role is that he's doing. However, when he does have a movie role that requires him to bulk up, wow! I really can't put it into words. If you could see the look on my face right now...

Oh my goodness, he is absolutely beautiful. Yes, I said beautiful. His aura illuminates any room that he walks into. It is mind boggling the way he commands attention without even saying a word.

Even with all of that, Blake is not arrogant, although he could be if he really wanted to. He has learned when to use his status and when not to. He's actually down to earth, likes to have fun and just be Blake... nothing more, nothing less; thus, he was definitely raised right.

He and his sister, Deadra, are very close. She is younger by three years, married and just had her first child, a daughter. Blake goes to see them as often as he can, as well. He loves kids and they certainly love him.

He had always told me that he was looking forward to having a big family.

As far as acting, Blake started out at a young age as he was unbelievably adorable as a kid. His parents were often told that they should try to get him into commercials. So, one day, his mom decided to do it and it was on from there.

At first, acting was just a way to get out of school on some days, but he soon fell in love with it. He realized and fully accepted that acting not football was his future. With all of that being said, he still went to college.

College, you ask? Yes, Blake went to college. He wanted to have that memorable experience with an historically black university. After graduating with a Business degree and a minor in Fine Arts, he moved to California, L.A. to be exact, to put forth more effort in furthering his acting career. It didn't come easy or shall I say all at once. Each role that he has had thus far seems to have built upon the other. They were just steppingstones for who he has become and what everyone sees now.

Blake is more than just a 'pretty face.' To be iconic in so many ways is how he wants to be remembered. Directors and others started to realize that he definitely had what it took to do so. Although he has been acting for several years now, for him, it feels like the last few years have been a steady climb to the top of Mt. Everest that he has yet to reach... so he says. In all honesty, I don't think he'd even be content then. That's just the kind of ambition he has.

As I mentioned, as I child, he dreamed of playing professional football. I think just about every child dreamed of being the one who caught the winning touchdown or got the game clenching interception... you know, just being a hero in some capacity.

Blake is definitely hard on himself about whatever he does; thus, he is NEVER satisfied. He's always trying to figure out what else he can do to reach that next level. Now, he feels that it's not just about him.

It's about his family, his family to be, those around him and those coming up now and after them.

He feels strongly about being able to pave the way for young people and provide an avenue or an alternative for them that they wouldn't normally have. Therefore, Blake has started a nonprofit to try to open doors that many would see closed. In addition, he has invested in other areas outside of acting plus a spot for a production company is now in the works.

Now, let's get to the somewhat *(I'm side-eyeing right now)* good part... Blake has had a few private relationships and a couple public ones, especially his last one. Her name was Aasira who definitely did not look her age of 36. She was absolutely stunning and the daughter of a well-known business mogul who owned a hotel chain that Blake had always admired.

Everything about her was always on point. Aasira was known for being an influencer on all social media outlets. Everyone wanted to know what she was doing or *who* she was doing at all times. She didn't mind it because she loved the attention. They had met before, but both of them were involved with someone else back then. However, this time was different. They were both single now and the opportunity to get to know each other presented itself again.

The weekend was finally here. It was a pre-party of an awards show on a beautiful, Friday night. All the high profile celebrities were there which meant Aasira would be, too. She wouldn't have missed it for anything. I mean, in order for you to be the bubble, you have to blow it up, right?!

Blake saw her from across the room and was instantly fascinated by her beauty again as if he had never seen her before. Her hair was in a sleek, side ponytail style accentuating her face. Her dress was silky and black showing her midriff with a side-split that seemed to be a mile long.

"Aye, I'll be right back. I see someone that I need to talk to right quick," Blake said to his friend, Deuce, as he hurriedly walked away. He

slowed down as he neared closer trying to give off a calm, cool, collected presence.

Aasira had her back turned towards him. Smoothly, he said, "Excuse me, Aasira, right?"

"Yes, that's correct, and you are?" Aasira said teasingly.

Blake raised an eyebrow as if to say, 'you mean you don't know who I am?'

Before he spoke, she said, "I'm just kidding. I know who you are." They both laughed.

With a little side-eye, Blake said, "Oh ok." He continued to speak and change the subject. "Are you here with someone?"

"Just a couple friends who you probably know," she said as she pointed them out. They waved back at her smiling widely.

"Oh yeah...most definitely. Do you, uh, wanna get out of here?" Aasira nodded with a mischievous look, and they left the party... together.

From that moment on, Blake and Aasira were an item. They were labeled

the 'IT' couple. Social media loved to
see what they were up to every day
because that's what she was all about.
Attention really should have been her
first name.

Blake wasn't the one for all of
the public hoopla, but he loved her.
So, he said 'why not.' After about a
year (really before that), Blake
started to believe that Aasira was the
one and wanted to settle down and get
married. At first, she was all in. They
looked for houses together, rings, etc.

However, there was one thing that
Blake mentioned that didn't quite sit
well with her... prenup. For a while,
she really considered signing it but
began listening to friends and some of
her family members. They would tell her
that if Blake really loved her then a
prenup was not needed.

Blake still proposed to Aasira.
She said 'yes' even though she knew
deep down that she wasn't going to sign
the prenup. She thought maybe he would
change his mind about it; thus, they
started to have more and more
disagreements.

Eventually, he gave her an ultimatum: sign the prenup or part ways. There was really no need to keep things going if she wasn't going to sign it. After all of the back-and-forths and arguments, Aasira decided that she would end the relationship. She realized that Blake wasn't going to change his mind about it, nor was she.

When it came down to it, she felt that she had a lot more life to live. Settling down would mean that she would have to give up so much. Being his wife meant that she would be nothing more in her eyes and more importantly anyone else's.

This breakup was hard on him; thus, he vowed that the next time he was in a relationship that it would be as private as possible. He was very hurt by the whole situation. There were other red flags before the breakup. However, he ignored them because he loved her that much.

Thankfully, Blake had a TV show that he was currently shooting plus a lot of other work in the pipeline that kept him busy through it all. His focus and determination became more intense

following that day. He did become
isolated for a couple months after that
because he needed that time for
himself... to reflect... to regroup...
to let her go.

He did everything he could to try
to move on and be content with just
himself without her. Blake did some
much needed and welcomed traveling and
attended several different events. He
realized that there were still people
he hadn't met plus things he hadn't
done, seen or experienced himself.
Thus, it became more apparent that it
was the right decision not only for her
but for him, as well.

Not too long after the
relationship ended with Aasira, he
remembered someone he had met during a
break while promoting a movie. It was
at a poetry club that he went to with
his team. However, that night was not
the first time he had seen 'her.'
Several months before that in
Philadelphia, Blake saw 'her' at
another poetry event. From that very
moment, he always had 'her' in the back
of his mind.

Ok, now this is the GOOD part. This is how that night went with a lot of input from what Blake told me on our first official date...

It was a cool, breezy, Fall Friday night in Philadelphia around 7:00pm. Blake was in town putting in work with his team. They had heard about how huge the poetry scene in the area was. So, they wanted to go check it out and just have a little fun away from promoting the movie. Blake, of course, agreed to step out with them, to see what all the hype was about. He has a wide variety of interests and poetry was definitely one of them.

When they walked in, it was basically a full house. There were two levels. Blake and his group sat on the upper one to not cause a distraction. The way the place was set up allowed for any seat to see the stage perfectly at any angle. There was a house band and several poets who had already performed. One had just finished when they walked in. It was time for an interlude which allowed the house band to set the mood even more for the night.

The whole crew ordered drinks and chatted about everything that had happened on the trip, thus far.

While bobbing to the music, Blake said, "This band is fi!"

Agreeing with Blake, Deuce said, "Yes, it is!"

After about 15 minutes, the MC came to the stage. The band started to play softer in the background. "Are ya'll enjoying yourselves?"

"Yeah!" the crowd yelled.

"I said, 'are ya'll enjoying yourselves?!'" the MC repeated.

"Yeaaahhh!" the crowd yelled even louder.

"Well, coming to the stage right now is an up and coming poet. It's her first time here. So, show her some love, ya'll. Coming all the way from Vegas by way of Tennessee. Show some love for, Nef-er-ti-ti!" The crowd proceeded to clap loudly.

She walked on stage and said nervously, "How's everybody doing tonight?"

"Good!"

"Ok, so this poem that I am going to do is from my first book," she said this as she was holding up the book.

"At any time after I get off the stage, you can come to my table over here on the right side (spotlight shines on her table to show the crowd) to get a copy. Thank you in advance. This poem is called 'Knock...'"

She paused for a moment and started...

With a passionate stare into your eyes
I silently sigh
Because you do not realize
How much love I have inside
Of me
For you
Your very presence causing an emotional and physical
uproar
That I try to hide
Because I fear your reaction
And what would happen
If I told you that I wanted to be in your life
I fear the rejection and the humiliation that I
might feel
Because of what I could reveal
Hurting my pride

But still…

Wanting to cause a sudden blush or smile on your face
I innocently wave and quickly look away
And then with a seductive walk
Glide pass you
Hoping that whenever you see my hips
You feel the same way as I do
Wanting you to take a sip
From the very faucet that drips
With just one word from your lips
But still…
It's a trip
Because…
With all of the pain and heartache that I've known before
To you, my heart would open its doors
If you would just…
Knock.

Normally, when the crowd really liked a poem, they would just snap their fingers as loud as they could, but this time was different for them and for her. It started with snapping and then changed to clapping and cheering. She was completely overwhelmed and beyond happy. You could tell by her expression that it felt really, really good to have that type of reaction.

"Thank you. Thank you so much!"

She went back to her seat and hoped many of them would come to the table to purchase a book.

Little did she know that during the poem this was happening...

When she got on stage, Blake said, "Damn. She is beautiful."

One of his assistants said, "Uhm, Blake, you are taken."

"Yeah, but I still have eyes. Oh... my... goodness," Blake said looking mesmerized.

When she started to talk, he became even more intrigued by her. "Her voice is so angelic. Wow!"

"Yo, snap out of it!" said Deuce while popping Blake on the side of the head.

Laughing, Blake said, "Alright, alright, I'm back," even though, he really wasn't.

While reciting her poem, he looked at her as if he was already taking her soul and putting it in his pocket for safe keeping. The thing is she actually felt something like a chill while on stage but didn't know what the heck it was.

Deuce noticed this look that was still on Blake's face and nudged him. Leaning over to Blake, "Maaaann, what's up?! I know that look, man. What's up?"

He smiled and said, "Nothing. Just make sure you follow her on all social media accounts that she has."

"Done," said Deuce as he gave a thumbs up.

After a moment, Deuce said, "Hey, Blake, guess what?! She'll be in Atlanta in a few months. I think that's around the same time you are filming, correct?"

"Yes. Yes, it is. Thank you, dawg." Blake made a mental note to put this on the calendar to go to.

BIRTHDAY MODE

It's my birthday weekend! So, I decided what better way to celebrate it than to go see my best friend, Naquita, who lives in New York.

I slowly opened my eyes as I sensed the lights come on. The flight attendant began instructing us to ensure that our seatbelts were fastened, because we were about to land.

After we touched down, I texted her as soon as I could to let her know that I made it and couldn't wait to see her. It had always been her dream to be in New York and she has certainly fulfilled it. Naquita is one of the top lawyers in the state and married with two daughters. We have been friends since college which was almost 17 years ago. So, yes, that makes me about to be 38, but I don't look it for sure.

When I got off the plane, I didn't have to go to baggage claim. So, I went towards the exit to look for a cab. There was one available as soon as I walked out of the lobby looking for it. Luckily, I was able to get a young lady who was very nice and helpful. Her name was Aphrodite.

During the ride, we had a great conversation. She gave me the inside scoop on all the hot spots for poetry, soul food and shopping that was close to downtown. I told her that I was in town visiting a friend and that it was my birthday weekend. The ride didn't seem as long as it actually was since we were talking nonstop. I gave her a $30 tip, a signed copy of my book and a great review.

When I walked into the hotel, it was basically empty. It was not surprising being that it was so late. I checked in and went up to my room as fast as I could. It was on the sixth floor with a city view per the website, but I didn't even go to the window to check it out. The first thing that caught my eye when I walked in was the huge bed as I just dropped my bag... not even trying to put anything away right then or shower. I flopped down on it and fell fast asleep. Exhausted, I slept through the whole night in my clothes, no interruptions, no cover or anything. I was completely out for the count.

The next morning, I was awakened by the warm rays of the sun beaming through the window. When I realized that I slept in my clothes, I laughed and said out loud, "Whew, I was tired as hell!"

I sat up feeling refreshed and looked around at how beautiful the room was. It was absolutely breathtaking, even though it was not a suite. Yeah, I wanted to do it big for my birthday and be downtown with all the happenings.

As I mentioned, the room had a king size bed that was obviously very comfortable since I went right to sleep last night. The color scheme was shades of neutral hues with hints of blues and greens. The window view showed over downtown and all it had to offer. I was in heaven. The bathroom had a separate tub and shower. Then it had a separate room with a door for the toilet. There was a small living room area plus a kitchenette and wet bar. Yep, this was the LIFE!

I went back to the window and just stared outside. I enjoyed seeing all of the hustle and bustle that I saw. I

became even more excited that I decided
to come.

        I was knocked out of my trance by
my phone as it began to ring; it was
Naquita. As soon as I pressed the
'Answer' button, all I heard was,
"Girl, get your ass up. I am here in
the lobby. So, I hope you're ready?!
Come down here and get me."

        "Of course, I'm not! I slept with
my clothes on and literally just woke
up but I'm coming. I can't wait to see
ya!"

        I grabbed my room key and hurried
down to the lobby. As soon as we saw
each other, we yelled (hotel yell) and
hugged while smiling and laughing. It
was bittersweet to see her even though
it had only been a few months since we
last saw each other.

        "Get some clothes on... you know
I'm hungry," said Naquita.

        "Heck, I am, too!"

        We rushed to the elevator. While
riding up, she asked me if I had heard
from Blake. I told her that I would
show her the text he sent just
yesterday morning.

After I was done taking a shower and getting dressed, I showed Naquita the text. She, of course, gave me a speech about forgiving him. I quickly changed the subject to what we really needed to discuss – FOOD. Naquita and I decided to go to a breakfast spot around the corner that the driver from last night told me about.

Naquita grabbed our purses and we headed towards the elevator. As the doors opened in the lobby, I saw someone sitting at a table having a conversation with a lady who looked to be a reporter. As I got a little closer and he started standing up, I gasped and stopped dead in my tracks. It was him... Blake... Blake Lovingly.

Naquita saw the look of surprise and shock on my face and whispered, "What is wrong with you?! Why did you stop all of a sudden?! Wait! Hold... up! Girl, what?! What is it?!"

"Blake. Blake is over there." (I whispered.)

"Where?!"

"Ohhhhhhh, shit! Damn! The pictures still don't do him justice! Go over there and talk to him," whispered Naquita.

Blake looked to have just gotten a fresh cut and I almost got lost in the waves. On top of that, he was dressed in a black suit where the openness of the jacket exposed a white lower cut shirt and dangling figaro chain accentuating his pecks that peaked out just a little. The entire outfit was tailored to every bit of his chiseled physique that made me start to feel weak.

"No, I will not!" I said while trying to gain my composure.

"Well, looks like you don't have to anyway, because he's coming over here. Yesssss!" (Naquita said teasingly.)

I tried to move to go the other way, but Naquita blocked me and said, "Girrrrl!"

Here he comes flashing that sexy smile as his eyes still sparkled with every step. We haven't seen each other in a few months, that is not since New Orleans. I got so nervous seeing him. Here comes the butterflies.

At this moment, I couldn't say a word. I couldn't even move. I was literally frozen. As Blake walks up, he reaches for my hand and says in the smoothest, raspiest tone that was always hypnotizing, "Hi Nefertiti. How have you been?"

Then he smiled again. I thought to myself... *oh my God! Did I just faint?! Ok. I'm still upward*. He spoke to Naquita, and I think she was smiling wider than he was. Still speechless, Naquita nudged me, and I finally broke out of my trance as my voice cracked while saying, "H-hi Blake. I-I've been great. How about you?"

"Missing you... missing you a lot," Blake said as he stared into my eyes for a moment.

He then continued by saying, "So, is it alright if I call you later so we can meet up and talk? I have a couple of interviews this morning that I am scheduled to do, but I really need (*he paused while closing his eyes for a second*) ... and want to talk to you." Blake never beat around the bush with what he wanted. This was another trait that I loved about him.

Naquita nudged me again, "Uhm, I don- (she nudged me even harder) ... yes, yes you can."

Smiling again because he saw Naquita nudge me, he said, "Good! I still have the same 213 number. I know you probably deleted it or blocked it."

"I remember," I said nonchalantly while rolling my eyes which made him laugh.

"Ok, I'll call you in a few hours. Let me, uhh, let me get back." He said as he looked me up and down.

Blake then hugged me tightly for what seemed like forever as if to say, 'I'm not letting you go this time.' His cologne was the same one he had on the last time I saw him which made me easily drift back into a trance.

Whew! *That* weekend!

But anyway, like I said, it had been a while since I last saw him. As we were letting go, he kissed me on my forehead, and I almost melted like an inflamed candle. Then he said, "See you later, baby."

While watching him walk away, Naquita and I glanced at each other. His walk was something else about him that was beyond sexy. It exuded confidence in every step that would make anyone swoon. It also screamed "Big D" energy in which I **already** knew about.

Our eyes were as wide as Bo Dollars screaming to ourselves, 'Got damn!'

We watched him until he got back to his seat. As if he knew I was still looking at him, Blake looked over at me and gave me a wink. It still had the same effect. HE still had the same effect on me.

Naquita and I started walking towards the hotel exit to get breakfast. "Girl, am I walking normally?"

"Yeah, why did you ask me that?!"

"Ok. No reason... just checking."

I asked her that because it didn't feel like it to me. It felt like I was wobbling. My legs felt rubbery as the memories of our time together started replaying in my head. Oh my goodness!

As soon as our feet touched the street, she said, "So, are you finally gonna tell me ALLLLL about how ya'll ended up here at this moment?"

"Yes, I'll fill you in when we are able to sit down, because I am going to need a seat... for real."

We made it to the restaurant in about 7 minutes. There was no wait time even though it was busy. It seemed like that one available booth was waiting for us. So, we seated immediately which was perfect since we were both starving.

The restaurant reminded me of some places back home in Tennessee. The smell had my mouth watering big time. Our waiter came to our booth about two minutes later and introduced himself telling us about their breakfast specials plus take our drink order.

As soon as he left, Naquita started in on me asking questions. "Oook, sooo... start talking! Don't you leave out not na'an detail either... and I mean na'an!"

I laughed and said, "Ok... ok. So, before I saw him in Vegas at a basketball game, I actually saw him twice before that.

"Wait?! What?!" said Naquita in a puzzling way.

"Yeah, I know. The first time was in Atlanta. Well, at least that's what I thought was the first time. He told me about the 'official first time' when we had our first date." I paused to take a sip of orange juice and then continued...

"Blake was in town filming and just so happen to decide (so I thought) to go to a poetry spot with some co-workers. Yes, it was the one night I was in Atlanta to do some poetry from my book... you know for promotion. It was my turn to take the stage. I was ninth out of the eighteen poets that were to perform."

"What poem did you do?"

"I did... THAT WORD."

"Oh, no you didn't?! That was definitely the perfect one."

"Yeah, I sold out of the books I had and got several online orders after that. It was a great night."

Just in case you were wondering, the poem goes like this...

you are held captive by my voice

as i am whispering
the sweat oozes out of your pores
and your forehead is glistening
because everything i say
caresses your eardrum
like a gentle breeze
while making you weak in the knees
then causing the blood in your body to vibrate
as if it was an earthquake
while keeping your heart
dangling on a leash
as if each word was a jerk
that made it beat
then filling your emptiness
sending you to heavenly bliss
hindering you powerless
to the way it saturates
overflowing your mind
time after time
you are spellbound
paralyzed
by each syllable's sound
as you sit on the edge of your seat
wanting me to repeat
that...
word...

"I was on cloud nine because the crowd loved it. It was beyond my wildest dreams. I was smiling from ear to ear. Blake was actually the last one to sit down... staring... not taking his eyes off of me. It was captivating, the way he looked at me, because somehow, I could feel his eyes even though I didn't know he was there. I didn't realize it at the time until now that I was already under his spell."

Naquita was so immersed in our conversation. With bright eyes, she said, "What do you mean?"

"From what he said, the way he was looking at me was not for the weak."

"So, did he buy a book or whatever? Did ya'll talk at all at that moment if he did?"

"After all were seated, I invited them again to... you know... come to the table where I was sitting to purchase a book if they were interested. It was perfect timing since it was about to be the intermission of the show."

"Blake was with a couple of his castmates (as I said earlier) and they peeped out how he was staring at me. He

told me this when we finally had a
conversation in Vegas (the third time
we met). Blake was actually in a very
public relationship at the time, as we
all knew."

"Oh, yes, we knew... heifer."

I laughed so loud, "What you
said?!"

We both chuckled again.

"Ok, now keep talking," said
Naquita still intrigued as if we just
started the conversation. "Did he get a
book, a number, or what?!

"Yes, Blake came by the table. I
had my head down. What made me look up
was the scent of his cologne. It smelt
so good. The kind that made you stop
whatever you were doing and just take
in the moment... which I did every time
I saw him. When I looked up and saw
that it was him, he said, "Hi, I'm Bl-
..."

"Blake Lovingly," I said.

With a huge smile, he said, "Yes,
that's me."

To Naquita, I described his
silhouette, "His dimples were like
pools with deep depths that I wanted to
drown in. His eyes were glistening in

the light from my table lamp, and I was smitten already. I tried my best to not let him see that. However, he told me otherwise later."

The waiter brought out our food and we continued to talk as we ate. I told Naquita that Blake just told me that he really enjoyed my poem and would love to purchase the entire book. He told me that I have a unique style and loved every word that he heard which made him 'want to hear... read more.' I signed it and gave it to him. He shook my hand and held it a bit longer than a normal handshake... but there was no more than that."

"Well, shit!"

"That's what I said to myself! He was in a relationship. So, I definitely was not expecting anything; plus, I mean he is Blake Lovingly. So, I was sure that he could have whoever he wanted whenever."

Naquita and I laughed again. "Ok, so tell me about the second time ya'll met... the alleged second time."

"Alright, it was, of course, at a poetry spot but this time it was in L.A. You know that's where he lives. I decided not to fly in from Vegas but drive instead. It was a beautiful scenic route and much needed me time. I even stopped a few times to take some pictures and just breathe the fresh air."

"Oh, so, this is the spot that you are always telling me about, then."

"Yes, that's it."

"Nice," Naquita said as she took another bite.

"Yeah, but this time he was with his girlfriend. I could tell that she didn't want to be there but just went because he wanted to go." I paused.

We both looked at each other while rolling our eyes and said, "Being supportive," and laughed.

"So, so, what poem did you do at this one?"

"I did 'Poetry (to me)' that night."

"Oh yes, again, perfect timing because she was there with him. How did that go again?"

"Well, let's see...It went like this...

Your warmth
Awakes me every morning
Like the delicate touch
Of a feather upon the skin
Teasing me
As I am overcome
With so much fire
Exuding
With so much emotion
That I have no choice
But to give in
Causing my spirit
My soul
To emanate
As I anticipate
The numbing sereneness
Of your gift
As your every stroke
Sends me on a long voyage
Causing me to drift
Into a seemingly never-ending
Hypnotic state of
E--la--tion
Mentally drowning
As I stagger
Because of your in--tox--i--ca--tion
Constantly keeping me in a daze
Due to the many
Meticulous
Elaborate ways
That you cause my ink

To spill
And formulate
In each and every way
The pleasures you give
On every single page

"Oh yeah, I bet he loved that one!" Naquita shouted.

"I actually didn't see him until I got on stage which was crazy. I got nervous and hadn't been like that in a long time."

"Awww, he made you nervous... so cute."

"Yes, he did but I played it off and did my thang." We laughed. "When I finished, I received an overwhelming response. Once more, he was among the last to sit down even though Aasira was with him."

"I bet Miss Thang didn't like that, huh."

"Of course not, but I sure did. Again, he came over to the table but with her this time and bought another book. He told her that he saw me in Atlanta at a poetry club. She was so uninterested, but Blake was and that was all that mattered to me."

"Let me get one f-..."

Aasira interrupted him, "I thought you already had one."

Blake said, "Yes, I do but I want to give this one to my sister. So, Nefertiti, just sign it to her for me, please. Her name is Deadra."

I signed the book and gave it to him. He told me to keep writing and performing as he flashed that mesmerizing smile. All I could think of was being in a pool, but he was spoken for. So, I didn't go towards the deep end. I just stayed in the shallow end by myself... wading.

Naquita and I finally got done eating. We were on the midst of having the I-TIS because the food was so good, plus, the portions were hefty. We were beyond full. I, of course, had turkey bacon, French toast, hashbrowns and eggs. Naquita had sausage, an omelet, hashbrowns and French Toast. We decided to make a couple blocks to walk the food down before heading back to the hotel. That way we could continue to catch up and chill.

As we were walking back, my phone rang. I hesitantly looked at it to see the number. It was Blake! I looked at Naquita.

"Girl, if you don't answer that damn phone; I will call your mother!"

I answered, "Hello."

"Hey, it's me, Blake. I didn't think you were going to answer, but I am certainly happy you did. Are you still available to talk later?"

"Yes. Yes, I am."

"Ok great. I am actually staying in the same hotel. Looking at my watch, I see it's about 11:30. Can I come see you around 2:30 or so? Is that alright?"

"Let me check with Naquita to see if that's ok because we were about to..."

She interrupted me and yelled, "No, we can do it tomorrow, Blake! She's FREE the rest... of... the... day!"

"Yes, Blake. That's fine."

"Good. Like I said, I miss you, Nefertiti. Please text me your room number. Thank you Naquita!" Blake yelled at the end so that she could hear him.

"You're welcome!" Naquita yelled back.

I rolled my eyes at her and continued talking to Blake. "Ok, I will as soon as we end the call."

"Bet!" he exclaimed.

We hung up. "Girl, why did you..."

"No, ya'll need to talk. Shit! Plus, I want to hear what happened in Vegas because obviously what happened in Vegas didn't stay and it's here in New York! I KNOW you left out some details when we talked a few months ago."

"Weeellll, I might have left out a few."

I then texted Blake the room number.

'Thank you. I'll see you soon. I love you,' he replied but I didn't.

REMINISCING

Naquita and I arrived back at the hotel and went up to my room. That walk around the block really helped. Our I-TIS was gone but we were still full. The whole time we were there, we laughed and talked like we were still in college.

Naquita said, "Don't avoid it, now. Tell me what happened when ya'll met in Vegas! Again, don't leave not na'an detail out either! Not na'an..."

"Al-right, al-right. Well, you know I love the women's professional basketball team there and go to the games as often as I can. So, it was a Thursday night, I decided to go to the game at the last minute. I thought I would be too tired after work but surprisingly I wasn't. Then I searched online to see if anything was available. Luckily, there was a seat left in my favorite section."

"Ok, get to the part where you see him."

Giving Naquita a side-eye, I say, "Look, you said not to leave not one detail out."

"I said na'an but keep talking... starting with when ya'll saw each other."

"Well, it was about two minutes left in the second quarter before half time. I started looking around for some reason. Something was like, 'hey, girl, you need to look up right there.' So, when I did look up, I saw him and was completely caught off guard. To myself, I said 'oh my goodness... what is he doing here'. He was sitting in the box seat right above my section with a few friends. Blake didn't see me look up but his friend, Deuce, did. He told me later on how the conversation went..."

"Yo, Blake... man if you don't stop staring at this girl and ask her to come up here! Damn! I bet you haven't looked at the game at all, have you? Hold up! Is that the poet from Philadelphia and Atlanta?!"

Blake gave Deuce a look and said, "Yeah, that's her. I can't believe she's here. Wow! Hold on, it's about to be halftime. So, I'll catch her when she is walking up this way."

Deuce yelled, "Maaaaann, hell naw... shit! I gotcha!" He got up and started walking out of the suite.

Blake was like, "Bruh! Deuce!" Deuce ignored him and proceeded to come my way.

I didn't come with anyone to the game; therefore, I was sitting alone. However, the people next to me were very friendly and chatty. We talked and laughed the whole first half. One of them had just got up to get some food when Deuce made it to me.

"Hi! Nefertiti, right? I'm Deuce. It seems that uh you and my boy up there..." (he points to Blake who's watching and gives the 'Whassup' nod and waved)

"...seem to know each other."

"I've seen him a couple times at some poetry spots where I performed but that was basically it."

"Well, apparently, you made a huge impression on him. He has been staring at you the whole damn first half. I don't even think he knows what the score is. I came down here to ask if you would come up there with us so ya'll can get to know each other. He

told me that there was a definite
mutual vibe between ya'll. As, the
world knows, he is a single man now.
No, he didn't send me down here to talk
to you. I just got tired of him staring
at you. So, what do you think? Will you
come?"

Hesitantly, I say, "I... I guess
so... why not?! He's right. There was a
vibe. Just so you know, I'm not one of
those little groupies or anything like
that who he may be used to or
whatever."

"Oh, he knows, believe me," Deuce
said with a 'you go girl' smile. He
stayed behind to talk to the girl that
was sitting beside me.

As I was getting up, he said, "Oh,
yeah, if you were wanting to grab a
bite during halftime, there's plenty of
food up there."

"Ok, great. Thank you, Deuce." I
looked up and Blake was watching me
walk up the stairs with a look that
made my whole body feel flushed.

So, I get there and he's standing
at the door waiting for me. "Hi,
Nefertiti. How have you been?"

"Hi, Blake. Well and you?"

"Wonderful! Especially now," he said as he gave me a huge hug. *"What are the odds of us both being here tonight, huh?!"*

"You've got that right!"

"Nefertiti, you strike me as a woman who loves to eat like I do. So, here's our spread. What do you want, and I'll fix it for you?"

"Oh, ok, thank you and you're right. I do." I told him what I wanted, and he did just as he said he would. He made his plate, too, of course. There were wings, rotel, spinach and artichoke dip, chips, fries, pizza, cookies and cake.

We started talking, *"The first few times I saw you were at a poetry spot. When did you start writing and why if you don't mind me asking?"*

I told him that I started in elementary school. My great aunt (God rest her soul) introduced me to poetry at an early age, and it was on from there... never looked back.

So, I asked him a deep question, as well. *"What made you want to be an actor?"* He told me that it certainly wasn't his first love so-to-speak. He *did some commercials and small acting jobs when he was younger. Blake was like 5 or 6 when he started and didn't know what he wanted to be at the time, of course.*

Around 12 or 13, he had his heart set on playing football professionally. But after a while, acting started to grow on him, in a manner of speaking. He started to realize his vision and kept at it; so, he moved to L.A. after college. There were times where he wanted to give up and wanted to just go back to New York or Seattle but didn't.

"So, girl, as you can see, we definitely had a whole vibe of our own that was very strong already and continued to grow that night. We ate and talked the whole second half!" (I smiled so hard remembering the feeling that I had just being around him.)

"When the game was over, he offered to accompany me to my car since I was by myself. He had his driver pick us up so that we could be 'sort of' alone."

"Uhh, where was Deuce?"

"Naquita, this mane was hollering at the girl who was sitting beside me, and they went off together somewhere."

So, the driver picked us up and we headed to my car. We had previously exchanged numbers before leaving the arena. I had parked at a nearby restaurant since I normally would get a bite there after games. However, I didn't have to this time.

We arrived at my car, and he got out with me to say goodbye. As I was getting my keys out of my purse, I dropped them on the ground. We both attempted to pick them up and Blake grabbed my hand as I grabbed the keys. We slowly stood up looking at each other. With his other hand, he intently grabbed my face and proceeded to kiss me.

"Was there tongue?" Naquita asked.

"No, not at first, but then he did subtly. When I tell you I had never felt anything like that before in my life. Wheeeewwww! I mean it!"

"Who stopped who?"

"Actually, his driver, which is also his bodyguard, because we were in another car's way."

Blake said, "I really enjoyed talking to you tonight. Will you accompany me to that Café over there tomorrow night around 7ish so that we can continue our conversation? I want to know even more about you. You are truly, truly one of a kind."
Shyly, I said, "Uhm, so did I. So yes, I will MEET you there."
Blake told me that he loved to go to this spot whenever he was in town. After agreeing to see him, we kissed again before I got in my car.

"Ok. Let's fast forward to the next night," Naquita said excitedly while hitting the bed.
"Well, as I said earlier, I told him that I would meet him there since it was only ten minutes away from my house; plus, I didn't know him like that, yet. I didn't care who he was; although, it felt like I had known him my whole life already. How is that?! It was almost too much for me to accept.

How could I have these types of feelings for him so soon? I told myself that I wouldn't over think it and would just go with the flow."

We were supposed to meet up around 7:00pm. So, I left about 6:30 to make sure I had enough time to park. Every night was busy in Vegas but especially Friday nights in that area.
It was about 6:50pm when I was walking up to the restaurant. The greeter said, "Hello! Thank you for returning to our Café'!"
(I go here often myself. So, they already knew who I was when I walked up.)
"Mr. Lovingly is waiting on you. Please follow me."
So, I followed the greeter who I've seen quite often named Sam. He guided me to the back of the restaurant where I had never been before now. It was an intimate area with a full bar, round tables with bar chairs and booths plus a stage for a band. Blake was sitting in a booth not too far from the bar area.

"Mr. Lovingly, your guest has arrived."

Blake stood up with his arms out as I approached him. He gave me a full body hug as if he loved me already, as if he would be my protector from this point on... nothing formed against me shall prosper in any way is how he made me feel already.

"Hi, Blake, you look very..." I paused because he looked like he just came from a magazine shoot... khaki linen pants and button down that was partially open to a black shirt underneath.

"What?! Like you want to take me home already?!"

I laughed and said, "You know what..."

"That I'm right..." he replied with a confident grin and raised eyebrow that made me suddenly lose my breath for a moment. I couldn't even say a word out loud after that statement. However, to myself, I said, 'Yes, you are definitely right.'

Blake then said, "You look absolutely stunning! Damn!" I had on a fitted backless, black, halter dress that came just below my knees that was not overly tight but accentuated every single curve with black stiletto heels (toes out). Yeah, I knew what I was doing, because last night he didn't see ALL this. At the game, I had on a black tank with a black, long sleeved, off-the-shoulder fish net top, wide leg, light-colored jeans and black sneakers. Going to the games, I need to be comfortable. I'm not trying to fall down because I'm clumsy. I can still be cute without heels in the arena. You know what I mean.

Blake gave me a gentle kiss on the lips as we sat down. The waiter came over and brought some red wine and water.

As the waiter was placing our drinks on the table, Blake said, "I went ahead and ordered some wine for us. You strike me as a woman that IF she drinks likes to have something with a lot of flavor and sweetness. So, take a sip and let me know if I was right or not."

Impressed, I looked at him and took a sip. I was blown away, again speechless. This man was definitely *doing a fine job of keeping me that way. But the thing was, I felt like this was just who he was... genuinely, attentive and intentional about everything when he's with someone that he really wants to be with.*

"You were exactly right, Blake. It was the perfect choice. How did you know?"

Blake said as he slowly licked his lips looking into my eyes, "...because I pay attention." He grabbed my hand and kissed it while still looking up at me.

"hmm... ok," I mumbled as I looked away...already wanting to just end the dinner right here and forget about eating. However, that thought quickly went away because it had been almost a year and a half since I had been with anyone.

"Look, I have to be honest with you. I saw you one other time at a poetry spot."

Surprised, I looked at him and said, "Really? Where was the other time?"

"It was actually the very first time I saw you which was in

Philadelphia." Blake told me about the night he saw me. I was shocked because the memory that I focused on was the feeling of a chill that I had all over my body at one point while reciting the poem.

Blake told me he was immediately blown away even though he was in a relationship. He said that he instantly felt a strong connection but didn't act on it, of course.

We stared at each other for a moment. It felt like we were on a secluded island in the middle of the Pacific Ocean. I was already his, but I couldn't let him know that. So, I pulled away and attempted to continue with our conversation.

"What's wrong?!" Blake said with a side grin.

I shook my head as if to say 'nothing' trying to ignore once again how he made me feel when our eyes locked.

STILL REMINISCING

I asked Blake, "So how long are you planning on staying in Vegas?"

"I'll be here until Monday evening. Then I'm flying back to L.A. I was told that you come here often when I mentioned your name. I had remembered you telling me that you love the food. They said that you always get one of three dishes. So, that's how I knew what to go ahead and order for the main course," Blake said after we were finished eating.

I just shook my head and smiled. "Don't think because you dotted all the i's and crossed all the t's that tonight will have a 'happy ending'."

"Oh, I'm not worried," he said while again flashing that sexy smile with a side of dimples and raised eyebrow as if to say, 'I know it will.'

Noticing that we were finished eating, the waiter came by and asked if we would like dessert. Blake chose a nine-layer chocolate mousse cake. I chose a slice of mango key lime cheesecake. The dessert was exceptional. As a connoisseur of cheesecake, I savored every bite. Blake noticed how I was eating the cheesecake, taking slow bites off of the fork. I could see him staring at me out of the corner of my eye which made me sensuously exaggerate the bites a little more. I was enjoying every minute of it trying not to let him know that I could see him biting his lip every time I took a bite.

We had finished eating about an hour ago. However, the conversation, the laughs, the gentle touches and occasional kisses between us were so good that we just kept it going. Not to mention that the restaurant had been closed for like 15 minutes... Surprisingly, they didn't disturb us until the very end when they were about to turn off the lights and close up for the night.

Since all guests were gone, we would be able to walk out the front of the building together with no issues. Just before leaving the restaurant, Blake said, "Let me text my driver to come through. Where did you park so that I can take you to your car?"

I had parked around the corner to the left in my usual area. While walking to my car, we were holding *hands and would look longingly into each other's eyes. No actual words were said, but the gaze could literally write a book.*

When we got to my car, I pushed the button to unlock it. Being a complete gentleman, he opened the door for me. When I turned around to look at him, he said, "I really had a wonderful time tonight. It's pretty late and uhm do you mind if I follow you JUST to ensure that you make it home safely?"

Before I could answer, his driver pulled up proceeding to hop out and open the passenger door for him.

Nervously, I finally responded, "Uhm, yes... yes, that's fine. As I told you, it's only ten minutes away."

"Ok. It's no problem at all." Blake paused for a moment and grabbed my hips. "You know I can tell you are nervous. I'm not going to try anything... unless you want me to." He said with a mischievous look while holding my hips more firmly.

All I could do was roll my eyes and he laughed out so loud. Blake and I got into our vehicles and headed to my house. He pulled right up behind me in the driveway and we both got out at the same time.

When Blake and I reached the front door, he said, "Again, I must say that I really had a wonderful time this evening. It feels like I've known you my whole life. I'm not just saying that either. It really does. We have a whole lot in common, many of the same wants, goals, desires and needs."

"Yeah, I know. It's crazy how..." Blake interrupted me with a kiss that made my knees buckle. He caught me and asked with a little laugh, "You, alright?"

Embarrassed as hell, I responded in a smart way, "Yes, I'm fine. Thank you."

"Can I come in for a moment and get a quick tour? I want to see if your decorations are what I think they would be... that is, if you don't mind."

I hesitated for a moment, then said, "Yes, you can come in for JUST a moment." (You ain't slick... I said to myself.)

We walked in and music started playing. Impressed, Blake said, "Wow!"

Looking at the expression on his face, I said, "Yes, I have a playlist set up to start when I walk in. I really love music... like old school soul, r&b, neosoul."

"That's a great idea. I might have to do that myself. I love it!" Blake said with a huge grin. I then gave him a tour of the rest of the house and the backyard.

I had been in my new house for about three months now. It sat on three acres (fenced in), 3 bedrooms, 3.5 baths, game/theatre room, office/gym with a huge spacious kitchen and inside pool with an extracting roof and tinted, sliding doors to the outside.

"So, you've shown me every room in the house, the pool, plus the outside and even the laundry room... except your bedroom. Why is that? Is it junky or something because you couldn't decide what to wear tonight?"

"No, Blake!" I said while shaking my head and laughing. "Come on..." In the back of my mind, I felt like this was still a setup, but I didn't care. He made me feel like HE was worth it if anything happened.

I showed him the bedroom and bathroom and he was blown away again with my color choices, furniture and wall art. "This is absolutely beautiful. I know I keep saying that, but the entire house really is. It's actually even better than I thought it would be. Did you decorate this yourself? You might need to change professions! Seriously."

"Oh wow, yes, I decorated the entire house. Thank you! I believe I told you earlier, I've been here for about three months now."

"Well, I guess, I better go," he said sadly. "I have an interview in the morning." *We left my bedroom walking towards the front door.*

While slyly rushing him down the hallway, I said, "Yeah, that's a good idea so that you can be bright eyed and bushy tailed."

We laughed as we approached the front door. He reached for the doorknob but quickly brought his hand back, paused for a moment and turned around. I was looking down, as usual seems like. So, he lightly grabbed my face and gently raised my head. Looking into my eyes, he then kissed me. It was so innocent at first. Then it turned into the most intimate you-know-you-want-this kiss I had ever had, even more than last night. As he brought me in closer, he started to kiss my neck and shoulders while his hand was holding the small of my back.

"Blake... Blake..."

"Yes. What is it, baby?"

"Blake, I-I have literally only known you for 24 hours. I can't... I-I-oh my goodness!"

He kissed me right above my heart and I almost changed my mind.

"...I can't... I can't do this right now. It's too soon."

He growled a little which made me want to take back what I had just said and uttered, "Actually, you've known me for a few months," he said with a side grin; then continued.

"Ok. Ok. I understand... I really do. You told me how long it's been, and I respect that more than you know."

I could tell that Blake meant what he said, but at the same time, he sounded so disappointed. Actually, I

was too, but I couldn't do it. I just
couldn't.

I've been in Vegas for a little
while but still had not been with
anyone. I mean I went out on a few
dates but that was it. There was
nothing promising or felt worth it...
until now.

He kissed me again. I opened the
door to let him out. With a wink, he
said, "I'll text you when I get back to
the room after I take a cold shower."

I shook my head.

His driver was still outside
waiting on him. Blake started walking
towards the SUV. I closed the door and
leaned back on it trying to decide if I
wanted to catch him before he left. In
a moment's thought, I told myself,
'Girl, ya'll are both grown, and it is
time to let someone in even if it is
only for a moment.'

I opened the door and Blake was
standing right there waiting for me. He
had already told his driver to give him
a few more minutes as if somehow, he
knew I was going to change my mind. He
was right.

"Blake... what if I didn't come back to the door?"

"Then I guess I would have been standing here looking stupid as hell." We both chuckled. "I just wanted to kiss you one more time before I left."

The kiss was so sensual and intense that I almost asked him to stay but I didn't. After we kissed for what seemed like an infinite amount of time, he left. I closed the door almost changing my mind again.

This time, I decided not to open it; even though, I most definitely wanted to. Looking out of my peephole, this time I saw him get in the SUV and leave. As they drove away, I watched until I couldn't see it anymore. Hoping that he would turn around and come back, I sat on the couch in the living room. But fortunately and unfortunately, he didn't. After about six minutes, I accepted the fact that he wasn't going to come back. I looked out of the peephole just in case but didn't see him. I then decided to take a shower.

As soon as I got finished, my phone dinged. It was Blake. 'Hey

Nefertiti. I just wanted to let you know that I made it back to my room and that I wanted to see you in the morning for breakfast. Is that ok?'

A huge smile came upon my face. I haven't had that in a while, not like that anyways... and it felt amazing. I texted him back... 'Glad to hear that you made it back safely. Yes, breakfast would be great. Is 9am good for you?'

He replied, 'Yes, that's perfect. I'll pick you up.'

With a mischievous grin, I replied, 'Well, how about I just make a masterpiece spread and we can eat here... what do you think? I don't just write and decorate ☺'

It took him a moment to answer which made me almost regret my previous text. But then all of a sudden, I received this reply, 'I'm sure you don't. Actually, that works for me. I'll be there, promptly at 9.'

"Hold up now?! Didn't y'all just have an intimate encounter?! You knew darn well where that breakfast was going to lead to."

"Honestly, Naquita, I was hoping it did."

"Unh, huh! Fast tail! Keep talking!" Naquita shouted.

Ok, so the next morning, I was up early around seven. I had already planned the menu out in my head the night before immediately after getting the confirmation from Blake. It consisted of turkey sausage, turkey bacon, eggs, hashbrowns, almond/wheat waffles, grits and a fruit medley (strawberries, pineapples, kiwi, grapes, honeydew melon, watermelon blueberries and cantaloupe).

I had everything ready at 8:40am. So, I decided to take a shower before he arrived. Of course, he showed up a few minutes early at 8:52.

With my house having some technology features, I can open and lock the doors from wherever I am with my phone. I was still in the shower nearing the end of my cleaning and the doorbell rang.

I looked at my phone to see that it was Blake and then said through the speaker, 'Good morning, Blake. I'm in the shower. Letting you in. Everything is ready.' I see him nod and wink at me.

The door unlocks and he walks in proceeding to go into the kitchen. After about six minutes, I came out of the bedroom to greet him. "Hi Blake.'

"Good morning, Beautiful," he says as he hugs me. Then he continues by saying, "hmm you smell so good."

Bringing me in closer hugging me tighter, Blake lightly kisses me on my cheek. I almost melted. He was dressed in a black fitted tee and jeans. I had on a two piece relaxed but fitted lounge set that had an off the shoulder top.

Blake said, "I already peeped 'the spread' and I must say that you definitely did your thang. I'm so hungry."

With a shy expression, I said, "I tried."

Smiling, I turned to load up our plates and softly demanded, "Have a seat at the table. I got you."

"Yes ma'am," Blake said with a smile as he sat down.

"*Damn, even the presentation is fi'!*" *He said as I placed his plate and bowl of fruit in front of him.*

"*Thank you, Blake! What do you want to drink?*"

"*O.J. is cool.*"

Before eating we prayed over the food. I wanted him to take the first bite to see his reaction. "*Wow! I'm beyond impressed, but I really expected nothing less to be honest.*"

He made me blush again with that statement. We continued eating and talking. "*I have a couple interviews today starting at one. They shouldn't take long. What are you doing around 4 or 5?*"

"*I don't have anything planned, Blake.*"

"*Good.*" *He received a text right after saying that and read it.* "*Well, isn't this great timing.*"

"*What is it if you don't mind me asking?*"

"*No, I don't. Both of my interviews got pushed to Monday at 11 and 2. So, that means I am 'all yours' the rest of the day.*" *As he said that, he took a sip of his orange juice not* taking his eyes off of me for not even a second. I could feel the tension growing between us at that very moment, and it made me start to get nervous. With wide eyes, I swallowed what I was chewing and took a huge gulp of juice. He saw that and chuckled a little.

"Baby, why do you look so nervous?"

"Nervous?! Wh-why do you think I'm nervous, Blake?" I said as I picked up our plates to put them in the dishwasher.

"Oh, no reason, no reason at all," he said teasingly. "Let me help you with that."

Blake got up from the table and helped me clean up. He put the last of the food that was left into the fridge. Then came behind me putting his hands on the sink trapping me.

He said, "I've put the leftovers in the fridge." He then lightly kissed my exposed shoulder directly on my tattoo.

"Blake..."

"Yes, what is it?" He said as he continued to kiss my shoulder up to the back of my neck. I moaned a little.

"Ohh, that must be a spot. Interesting," he whispered as he kissed the same area again.

This time it made me stop washing the last skillet. He turned me around and grabbed the towel to dry my hands as he longingly looked into my eyes.

Staring at me as if he wanted to taste every inch of me like I was that piece of chocolate cake he had at dinner last night, he said, "I don't want to be anywhere else but here with you."

Then he kissed my lips as he grabbed my waist. Easily picking me up, he carried me to the bedroom. Still kissing, we sat down on the edge of the bed. He paused for a moment, looked at me and said again, "I don't want to be anywhere else. I mean that."

Again, we started kissing as I put my hands under his shirt. I could feel every muscle flexing as he caressed and lightly gripped my thighs. I then grabbed the bottom of his shirt gently tugging to pull it off over his head. Blake then raised up my top and softly kissed my breasts. His tongue, his lips

paid close attention to the shape and
contour of each one.

He removed my shirt and pulled
back my hair to expose my neck to again
kiss as if he was about to suck the
life right out of me. And if he did, I
would not have tried to stop him. This
sent a sensation throughout my body
that made me gasp for air suddenly. It
was another spot that I didn't know
existed, but he found it... easily.

"Blake, do you have a..." His
kisses caused me to not finish my
sentence, but he knew what I was trying
to ask.

"Baby, I have it right here."
Then he raised me up a little to put on
the condom.

First of all, in my mind, I'm
like, 'when did he take off his pants
and when did he pull out a condom?'
After he slipped it on, he lowered me
back down slowly.

'Oh, my goodness!' I said to
myself. Even though my eyes were closed
at the moment, it still felt like they
were bucked in disbelief. Where in the
world did all of this come from? 'Damn!
Nef, girl what are you about to get

yourself into?! It doesn't matter! I NEED this! I WANT this!'

He wrapped his arms around me picking me up and laid me on the bed... slowly pulling down my pants, my panties and... teasing every part of me with each tug and kiss until they were completely off. He threw them on the floor and spread apart my legs as he was kissing my thighs... outside... inside... outside... inside... up to the crease of my hips.

Surprised, I moaned with such anticipation of what was about to happen. I could tell that he smiled while saying, "Hmmm, not just yet. I can't give you everything the first time, but I am DEFINITELY about to give you something else." Blake spoke those words like we were already each other's.

His actions certainly proved that as he got on top of me positioning himself to enter my velvet center. Blake gradually worked it in as his strokes were slow and deliberate to not hurt me. It had been a while, plus he was certainly 'blessed.' I got wetter and wetter with every stroke which made him get even deeper.

Worried but smiling, he asked, "Nef, baby, do you want me to stop?"

"No... no," I said breathlessly.

Then right at that moment, I felt a warm sensation start throughout my body that was not familiar as he discovered more and more spots that I never knew existed. As my back began to arch, he felt that I was about to climax and wrapped my legs around his waist. I was his blank piece of paper, and he was a brand new pen filled with ink that was about to spill and create a new verse.

He whispered in my ear, "Hold onto me. Keep your legs right there. That's it, baby. Let it out. Let... it... out," he continued with a deeper, whispering tone as he somehow found a newer depth with each word.

I did 'let it out' with no hesitation. He slowed back down not immediately stopping but making sure that I had 'got it all out'. Blake looked at me while letting my legs down. Seeing the look on my face, he asked, "Are you ok, baby?"

"Yes, Blake."

We started playing hide and go seek with our tongues as he started back with that methodical stroke. I could feel his heartbeat from below as his moans became louder.

"Shit!" he uttered.

The feeling that I just had engulfed me again. I started to reach another peak and so did he. My eyes got watery, and a single huge tear rolled down my face.

"Damn..." he said as he laid on top of me for a moment still inside. After a couple minutes, he slid out as he kissed me. Then he laid his head on my stomach as I caressed it. We easily fell asleep for a few minutes.

I suddenly woke up and said, "Blake, Blake, we need to take a shower."

"Yes, we do."

We showered together stealing kisses and touches in between washing. He finished and dried off before me. While I was still in the shower, I reminisced on what had just happened. I had never felt like that before. The way he looked at me... the way he touched me... the way he kissed me... they way he... oh my goodness!

He was sitting on the edge of the bed in a towel looking at his phone when I came out. When he saw me, he proceeded to remove the towel and get in the bed. There were no signs that made me think what we just shared was about to be a hit-it-and-quit-it type of experience.

I opened my drawer to find a shirt and panties until he stopped me. "No, Nef, don't put on anything. Just come here."

He reached his hands out to me as I started walking towards him. I laid in his arms, and we quickly drifted off. Neither of us really slept well the night before. He was too restless thinking about me just as I was him.

After a few hours, he opened his eyes before me and caressed my face gently to wake me up. My eyelids slowly opened to see him smiling. It was so bright... like the sun was right there shining directly in my face. "Nef, baby, I gotta go to this interview. One of them changed their mind and now want to do it. Big J is on the way to pick me up. He said he was walking to the truck now." He kissed my forehead.

"Ok, Blake."

"Baby, that was better than I could have ever imagined. You know you got me whipped already, right!"

"Blake!" I yelled with surprise.

"I'm just being honest." We both laughed. What little did he know was that I felt the same way.

He put on his clothes as I got up and put on a robe. He received a text from Big J saying that he had pulled up outside. I walked him to the door. He gave me a huge hug and kissed on the forehead, the tip of my nose, then lips. "I'll call you when I'm done. I'm not leaving until Monday evening."

I closed the door. As I was walking back, I wrapped my arms around myself because I could still feel him holding me. Smiling from ear to ear, I laid back down. As I pulled up my sheets and buried my head in the pillow, I could still smell his cologne. Intoxicated by the scent, I went fast asleep even though it was now in the middle of the day.

"Damn girl, no wonder you were so mad at him!" Naquita said with an ohhh weee look. "I just know you wrote something about this, didn't ya?!"

"Maybe, maybe not... girl, you know I did! It was called ECSTASY:

I wanna make love to your mind
With every single word
Causing your toes to curl
With every syllable heard
I wanna make your eyes roll
To the back of your head
As the melodic tone of my voice
Massages your brain
Like those black satin sheets
Caress your skin
As you lay on my bed
Putting you in a daze
Because of the many erotic ways
That you and I
Would play
Causing you to only think of me
Every hour
Every minute
Every second

Of the day
And night
Because in me…you will fall deep
Since I'm the one you've been looking for
Your whole life
The one you were born to seek
Your wife
And all those shoes you tried on before me
Don't even matter
Since I'm your perfectly fitting slipper
Making you the male version of Cinderella
See
I wanna put a permanent smile on your face
That no one could ever erase
Because you love
The way I smell
The way I taste
Causing you to give me
Every cent that you have
Like I was your personal wishing well
And of course
I would do the same
Laying it down in every way
As I tame
You
So that your soul will whisper my name
And your heart will feel no more pain
Because I removed all scars

Healing
You
With the words formed by my lips
Sending you on an endless journey
An ecstasy filled trip…

A BIG MISUNDERSTANDING

"Wow!" Naquita said with such eagerness to hear what else happened between us.

"Ok, so what started the bitterness between ya'll? I remember you saying that he was even there for your surgery after only a couple months of ya'll dealing with each other."

"Yeah, that's right. So, what had happened was..."

We were so smitten with each other. I even traveled with him out of the country when he went to scout places for an upcoming movie. Everything seemed so right with us already. I don't know; maybe it was just because it was new to the both of us or maybe it was just meant to be.

About seven weeks in, I had a doctor's appointment because of some pain that I had been feeling more frequently. This had started even before Blake and I began seeing each other. I found out that I had to have surgery to remove a fibroid that was growing on the outside of my uterus. I wanted to have a different type of procedure to remove it. However, due

*to the nature of mine in particular,
they said that it was riskier.*

*My doctor really believed that I
should have a hysterectomy, but I
didn't want to do that, just yet, since
I was only 37. I asked her if I could
just have the fibroid removed. She said
that it was possible but wouldn't know
for sure until she actually got inside
to perform the surgery. It was
scheduled to happen at 6:00am in a
month.*

"What did Blake say when you told
him about your surgery and the possible
outcome?"

"He was actually very supportive,
reassuring me that nothing would change
no matter what."

*Unfortunately, he would be out of
the country, thus, flying back home
that day. So, he asked his sister,
Deadra, to come so that she could give
him updates. Blake was scheduled to
arrive later on that evening. He said
that he would be there as soon as he
landed. He had changed his return
flight from L.A. to Vegas.*

The day of the surgery I was so nervous. His sister spent the night with me and took me to the hospital. My mom got dropped off so she could be there, too.

"I wish you would have told me. You know I would have been there for you."

"Girl, I know. I wasn't expecting you to fly all the way to Vegas from New York for my surgery. Definitely not... but you know that I appreciate it."

Naquita nodded and gave me a hug while saying, "Keep going..."

So, the surgery went well. My doctor was able to remove the fibroid and its stalk plus a small piece of my uterus where it grew from. Obviously, the surgery was experimental. However, I was only supposed to be off work for 4 weeks... no strenuous activities.

Blake's sister stayed the whole time with my mom keeping him updated while I was in surgery. They kept me overnight for observation. I told my mom to go home to get a good night's sleep because I felt ok. Deadra went with my mom to get some rest, too.

About 12:15am, I felt a kiss on my forehead that was waaay too familiar. I opened my eyes to see that it was Blake. "Hey baby, how are you?"

"Blaake... when did you...?"

"Shhh, go back to sleep. I'll be right here when you wake up... ok." Then he kissed me on the lips and caressed my head.

"Ok." I was back out immediately. Those painkillers had kicked in again. There was a couch in the room with a blanket and pillow. Blake sat down and removed his shoes. He was so tired, but he wanted to come that night no matter the time.

The next morning around 8:00am, Deadra and my mom walked in. Blake and I were still sleep. He immediately woke up and hugged them. I heard commotion and looked up to see everyone in the room. They asked how I was feeling and if I needed anything. It was almost breakfast time for the hospital. So, I was fine; just happy that they were there.

The following afternoon, the doctor said that everything looked good and released me at 2:22pm. I was to be on a strict schedule of what I could and could not do. We all got into Deadra's SUV and went to my house.

While walking to the front door, Blake was so attentive and gentle with me. He saw that I was struggling to walk a little. So, he picked me up and carried me to the bedroom. "Do you need anything, baby?"

"No, just you."

He smiled and said, "Of course, I will be right back."

Blake went to talk to my mom and Deadra while I tried to get comfortable. I heard their conversation getting louder as they were coming towards my bedroom. I thanked them for being there for me and gave them hugs.

"I'll take it from here, ladies." Blake fondly said with his chest out. Everyone laughed except for me because it hurt. "Sorry about that baby."

"It's ok, Blake," I said as I smiled at him.

He stayed with me for the first two weeks attentively looking after me.

In about a week, I was able to do more for myself even though he didn't want me to, just yet. After a couple weeks, I probably could have worked since I was mostly remote. However, I had plenty of PTO plus it was the doctor's orders. So, I used it.

During that time, I noticed that he was getting calls from the same number at different times of the day and night. He would walk out of the room to answer or just ignore it. This made me wonder, of course, who the hell it was. My intuition led me to believe that it was HER, his ex, Aasira.

I won't lie. She was absolutely gorgeous. Being that her mom was a famous businesswoman, the family was quite well-off. Her and Blake stayed together for nearly two years. It had ended a few months before we saw each other again in Vegas.

He really couldn't discuss the situation in great detail. However, he knew that he could trust me. So, Blake basically told me in bits and pieces. He wanted to settle down, but she didn't want to sign a pre-nup. At first, she did but he believes that her *family and/or her friends told her not to agree to it. Blake didn't want to jeopardize everything he had built and continued to build. Although everything seemed great, he understood that nothing is guaranteed. So, they ended their relationship.*

Blake didn't say those exact words but from what he said and how he said it, that's what I filled in the blanks with. He never exactly told me that I was wrong.

Blake had some speaking engagements and interviews in Atlanta coming up. This meant that he had to return home so that he could get better prepared with his staff. I was feeling much better and ensured him that I would be ok. At that moment, he received a text from HER again. I got a glimpse of it that read, 'What time is your flight so that I can pick you up?' There was more. However, I didn't get a chance to see it before he quickly put his phone in his pocket.

Nervously looking at me, he kissed and hugged me while saying goodbye. "Baby, I'll let you know when I land."

"Alright..." I said with a look in my eye that he was not used to seeing.

"Are you ok? What's wrong?"

"Nothing, Blake, nothing."

"Are you sure?"

"Yes, I'm sure," I said while rushing him off towards the car so that he could catch his flight.

I watched him drive off and hurried back in. When I closed the door, I started to cry, because somehow, I knew that this was the last time that I would see him.

A few hours later, he texted me saying that he had made it back to L.A. and asked if I was ok. My response was 'Good and yes.' That was it.

He replied with, "Baby, are you sure you're ok?"

"Yes," I replied.

"Great! I'll talk to ya later. Get some rest. I love you."

I didn't respond.

Since he didn't reply to her text about picking him up, Aasira just showed up at the airport. She was able to get the information from one of his staff members who never cared for me for some reason. She, of course, is no *longer employed with him after he found this out later.*

She was there when he got off the plane. Completely thrown off by her presence, Blake said, "Aasira, wh-what are you doing here?"

"Surprised to see me, huh... well, I came to pick you up and take you home so that we could talk. I know you got my texts."

"What is there to talk about?!" Blake softly shouted.

"Us," Aasira said.

She had on a tight red dress and matching heels. It was his favorite dress of hers and she knew that as she threw her hand on her hip.

"I still love you, Blake, and I want to work it out. I know you still love me, too. I don't know why you are looking around. There's no one else here to pick you up. I told them that I would. So, you might as well just let me take you home."

"Shit!" He said as he picked up his bag and followed her to the car. While they were heading to where she parked, a photographer snapped a pic of

them walking together. Blake wasn't aware of this, just yet.

The ride on the way to his house was completely silent. He didn't even look at Aasira once. He wondered what she was up to as he stared out of the window. They pulled into the garage, and he said, "Thank you for the ride." Then he got out of the car to get his bag.

"So, you not gon' invite me in?!"

"Now, why would I do that? It's over between us, remember."

"You really gonna actually say that and you see ALL of this," Aasira says as she gets out of the car posing. She then started walking towards him.

"Yeah, I am and..." Blake is stopped mid-sentence with a kiss. He quickly backed away from her. "Stop Aasira! Get in the car and go home!"

"But Blake, we need to talk... about... us," she says with a puppy dog look on her face that he could never resist, but it didn't work this time. Next thing you know, he's getting calls and texts about the picture that was leaked of him leaving the airport with Aasira.

"Oh yeah, I remember this because I called you and was like 'girl, have you seen this shit'!?"

"Right! I was so pissed and hurt at the same time. So, I texted him because I didn't want to talk to him at that moment."

The text read...
"'How could you do this, Blake? I thought we were ok. I thought we had something going that we both wanted but obviously I was wrong.'"

Blake immediately called me several times. I answered on the third call crying. "Baby, I'm sorry. Please let me explain what happened. Please."

Aasira was standing right there listening and smiling. In the background I hear, "Is that her, Blake?! Who is that, Blake? Is that her? Tell her that you are home with me right now! Tell her."

He tried to quietly shush her, but she kept talking.

"Oh my God?! Blake! Is she... oh my God?! I can't... I can't believe you would..."

"Nefertiti, please, wait... let me..."

Click!

He suddenly heard silence on the other end. I had hung up. He tried to call me back several times, but I didn't answer.

"Aasira, how could you?! I need you to leave right fucking now! Get the fuck out!"

"Blake..."

"I said get... the fuck... out!"

She finally left and Blake went in the house continuing to text and call me leaving voicemails. I didn't answer. I didn't respond. As far as I was concerned, we were over and that was that.

"Damn, Nef, that's messed up!"

"Yeah, I know."

"When did you find this out?"

"In the voicemails that he left that I finally listened to a couple weeks later. I had deleted the texts already without reading them."

OLD FLAME

Over the next few weeks, I had fully recovered from my surgery. Everything was back to normal, except there was no Blake. I would see more and more pics of them together plastered all over the internet. So, to me, the voicemails didn't matter anymore. There was obviously nothing ever between us in the first place if he could go back to her so easily. That's how seeing them together made me feel.

Finally, on one Thursday evening, I was tired of moping around the house. I remembered that it was poetry night at this popular spot that I frequently went to. So, I decided to venture out and have some much needed fun. I left the house about 7:30pm since it was only about 15 minutes away. I was dressed in a black, long sleeved, silk romper with black pumps. My hair was in its natural state but in a bun! Yeah, I was feeling cute this night. Ookkaaayyyyy!

The spot was nice and cozy just like back in my home state. I wasn't on the list to perform and tried to be

incognito, but of course, someone saw
me. So, I had to drop a few lines...
    "Hi everyone. How are ya'll doing
tonight. I wasn't really prepared to be
up here but here goes..." I said as the
crowd snapped their fingers to hype me
up.
    "This one is called 'It's Getting
Late...'"

you've got me going around in circles
not knowing where to go
which way to turn
because i can't stop thinking about
you
and
me
me
and
you
i just don't know what to do
since i can't seem to stop the way i feel for you
and i don't understand why
because it seems like every other day i cry
tears of frustration
of doubt
and somehow
deep down
i feel that i know the answer

but just too damn scared to ask the question
since you constantly keep me guessing
constantly on my heels
one day you'll realize that i was the only one
who was real
but now
to you
it's just a game
and you just wanna play
as i look into your eyes
i peer through their window
and feel the warmth of your rays
as i contemplate
over and over
how far to go
if i should open my do'
and let you fill this void
this emptiness
that plagues my heart
should i let you spread apart
my...
but i'm afraid
and
it's getting late...

    You know I couldn't do one without
the other. So, I also did "*It's too
late*" which goes like this...

it's getting late
and you're still not here
but he's whispering in my ear
telling me things that i wanna hear
because he knows that you're not right
sometimes leaving me all alone
shivering
in the middle of the night
but he wants to be there
when you're not
wanting to caress those spots
since you're always so tired
while he's always in the mood
ready and willing to be my "comfort food"
even though you tell me you love me everyday
your actions rarely speak louder than what you say
and i'm afraid
so confused
as i sit here wondering what i should do
but he's whispering in my ear
coming closer to me
so near
to the point where i can feel the vibration of his heartbeat
as the heat exudes from his body
but i'm afraid
and each minute you're gone
the memories of us dissipates

when i look into his eyes
i don't think of you anymore
as we fall to the floor
time passes
the sun rises
it's a new day
you turn the key and open the door
to emptiness
because now it's too late...

The crowd loved them both and gave me a standing ovation. To myself, I said, 'I could get used to this again'.

As I walked back to my seat, I felt a tap on the shoulder. It was Zyaire. I haven't seen him in over twelve years. He's still fine as ever... 6 foot 6, smooth, dark chocolate complexion, was always a dresser plus a beautiful smile to match and tonight didn't disappoint. Zyaire was still perfect just like I remembered with a slim but muscular build. Instead of a goatee, he had a full beard which made me do a double take.

"Nefertiti..." he shouted over the crowd noise so that I could hear him.

Still in disbelief, I mouthed, "Zyaire... Zyaire... is that really you?!"

"Yes! It's me... in the flesh." He leaned over closer to me so that I could hear him clearly and said, "What are you doing here in Vegas besides wowing the crowd?"

"I live here now... been here for almost two years. What are you doing here?" I asked, still in shock.

"I'm here for a conference and then going on vacation. So, I'll be here for about two weeks."

"Oh really?!"

"Yes, we need to catch up. Wanna grab a bite after this?" he asked.

"Uhm, sure... I could definitely eat," I said still staring at him.

"Here's an open seat next to me if you want to go ahead and get that conversation started," Zyaire said as he flashed that smile. His voice was still as deep and soothing with every syllable as ever.

He pulled out my seat and I sat down. We started talking about our

college days and what's been going on
in our lives lately. About 45 minutes
later, the poetry event ended, and we
decided to get some breakfast. The
restaurant was about 5 minutes away.
So, we just walked to it.

While we were waiting on our food,
he said, "I don't see a ring on your
finger. I remember you had gotten
married or might as well had been
married. What happened if you don't
mind me asking?"

"Wait, have you been keeping tabs
on me or something?"

"Well, we have mutual friends."

"Uhh huh, ok..." I said while
rolling my eyes.

We both laughed.

"At this moment, I'll just say
that it didn't work out and I have
always loved Vegas. So, I decided to
move here for a fresh start... new
beginnings... new chapters."

"Shit, ain't nothing wrong with
that. As you can see, I don't have a
ring either. I never got married but
have two boys."

"Honestly, Zyaire, I am not
surprised."

"Why do you say that?!"

"You seemed like a bit of a player back then. So..."

"Ohhhh, come on now! I think I just let an opportunity get by without ceasing the moment and no one ever compared to 'her'," Zyaire said as he sipped his tea giving me that 'I'm talking about you' look.

I couldn't do anything but nod and say ok. At that precise moment, the waitress came by with our food. She had perfect timing. It was about to get awkward.

We continued to talk while eating and just had a great time... two old friends catching up... nothing more... nothing less. When we finished, he paid for our meals.

"Zyaire, I better get home. I have a long day tomorrow. It was definitely good seeing you."

"Alright, I understand. Can I have your number so that we can link up some more while I'm here?"

"Uhm, sure."

We exchanged numbers as he walked me to my car. We gave each other a hug and I could certainly tell for sure *that he still had a gym membership. It was definitely nice to see him again.*

A couple days later, Zyaire called, "I finally have some free time, so I decided to call to see what you were doing later."

We had been mostly texting since we saw each other. "Yes, I'm free. Have you been to the new theater, yet?"

"No, I haven't. That would be perfect. Then maybe we can grab something to eat."

"Absolutely, this time will be my treat. No ifs, ands or butts."

"Yes ma'am!" He said sarcastically.

We decided to grab a bite to eat first. Then we went to the theater. The show and atmosphere was more than we could have ever imagined.

Later on, Zyaire and I walked along the Strip talking and laughing. We had a great time. At the end of the evening, Zyaire accompanied me to my car and asked, "So, can I see you tomorrow?"

"Sure. How about you come over and I'll cook dinner... soul food... all your favorites. Does that sound ok?"

"*Absolutely! Sunday dinner! Most definitely!*"

We both giggled. I had my head down looking for my keys. Zyaire was silent and I noticed. When I raised my head up, he leaned over and gave me a kiss. "I'll see you tomorrow. Do you mind if I come a little early so that I can see you in action?"

I chuckled, "No, I don't mind. I'll text you the address." I got in my car and pulled off. I looked back and he was waving. It was so cute.

The next morning, I went to the grocery store to pick up some additional items I needed to cook this immaculate meal that I wanted him to never forget. The menu was going to be fried chicken, baked mac-n-cheese, collard greens and sweet potatoes plus honey cornbread. The dessert was an old school yellow cake with chocolate icing... from scratch.

Zyaire came by about an hour early. He helped me with some of the mixing... like the cornbread and cake but most of it was done. I was just about to start frying the chicken so it would be hot and that was it. We sat down to eat.

He was amazed at the taste of everything. "Why aren't you a chef?! Wow!"

"I am a woman of many talents, Zyaire."

"I bet you are... indeed." He gave me a mischievous look and I returned the favor.

After dinner, we decided to watch a movie in the theater room and had dessert. About 45 minutes into it, we started kissing. Then out of nowhere, my doorbell rang.

"I wonder who that could be. I am certainly not expecting anyone. Zyaire, I'll be right back."

"Ok. I'll pause the movie until you come back." Zyaire paused the movie, even though, we didn't know what was going on in it at the moment.

I smiled and nodded while walking out of the room towards the front door. I yelled, "Who is it?!"

No one answered. So, I looked out of the peephole and saw that it was Blake. 'Oh my goodness!' I screamed to myself. The doorbell rang again.

I slowly opened the door with a surprised look and said, "Blake, what... what are you doing here?"

"You weren't answering any of my calls or texts. So, I came by in person to try to talk to you. I miss you, Nefertiti."

"Blake, there is nothing to discuss. Remember, you made your choice."

"You still didn't listen to my voicemails or read my texts, did you?" asked Blake.

"Yes, I listened to the voicemails but..."

"But what... you don't believe me do you, baby? I called you a couple days ago and also texted you that I would be in town."

"Blake..."

Hearing the tone of our voices before I could get out another word, Zyaire came around the corner and asked, "Is everything alright, Nef?"

"Nef?!" Blake said with angst. "Who the fuck is this?!" Blake was furious seeing Zyaire.

"I think it's time for you to leave, bruh. I'm here now," said Blake as he looked Zyaire up and down.

"Blake... stop it! Zyaire, I'm sorry about this. You don't have to leave. Blake is the one who is going to leave," I said as I looked at Blake annoyingly.

"No, I'm not. I'm staying right the fuck here." Blake said sternly as he continued to stare at Zyaire.

With a sly smirk, Zyaire said as he looked Blake up and down, "No, it's ok, Nef. You have my number. Thank you for the dinner. It was absolutely wonderful. Let me go get my to-go plate and I'll talk to you later."

Zyaire went to the kitchen to get his plate. The way Blake was looking at me, I could see the hurt in his eyes. He said, "Dinner?! What the fuck?!"

When Zyaire came back from the kitchen, he stared at Blake while giving me a kiss on the cheek and walked out. The look on Blake's face this time was something I had never seen before. He was so jealous.

When Zyaire left, Blake walked in further closing the door and said, "Who

was that motherfucka? Are you sleeping
with him?"

"Blake, what are you doing? Why
are you here? If I was sleeping with
him, that would be none of your damn
business."

"Better not be," Blake said as he
walked angrily into the living room.

"Whatever! As I said earlier, you
made your choice."

"Baby, I'm not," Blake lowered his
voice and continued with a calmer tone,
"I'm not with her. I know you listened
to my voicemails and heard me say what
happened. I have no reason to lie to
you. I wouldn't do that."

"So, what was with all the pics of
you and her together? Tell me that..."

"Ok. Look... about a week after
that you still wouldn't return my calls
or texts. I was hurt, too. So, yeah, I
started talking to her again to see if
maybe... if maybe I made a mistake. But
really, I was just angry and knew that
she would be easy. However, after not
even a week, I realized even more that
Aasira wasn't you and never would be."

Blake grabbed my face looking
into my eyes and said, "I realized...

how much I loved you. I didn't want to believe that I could love you that deeply so quickly, but it was true."

I started crying and yelled, "A week! A freakin' week, Blake!" I turned my back to him.

"Nefertiti, please don't cry. I didn't come over here to do that. I didn't come here to make you cry."

He grabbed my shoulder and slowly turned me around to wipe my tears. I pulled away and ran to the kitchen as he followed. When he caught up with me, he grabbed me from behind and held me close to him tightly.

Still sobbing, I said, "Don't..."

He turned me around and said, "Please, baby..."

I looked at him and was instantly held captive by his gaze as he started to kiss me. Moving me backwards against the kitchen island, he paused for a minute and gently pushed my hair out of my face. His hand loosely but firmly gripped the back of my neck. Pulling my head towards him, Blake started kissing me again.

Blake pulled up my dress slowly placing his hand inside my panties to test the waters. He slid them down dropping them at my feet as I unzipped his pants. Then he proceeded to pick me up and we became one, still fitting like a hand in glove. We were both breathing heavily as he sat me on the counter. His thrusts were as rhythmic as I remembered.

He unbuttoned his shirt still kissing me as he dropped his clothes to the floor. He removed my dress and said, "I miss you so much."

Still one, Blake picked me up off of the counter and carried me to the couch. He sat down with me as we were still passionately kissing. Then he laid me down resting a pillow under my head.

"I want you back." He said as he got deeper letting me know that nothing had changed... that I will always belong to him and he to me no matter what. Almost immediately, our moans became in full sync. He knew I was about to explode. So, he paused and looked at me slightly pulling out.

"Blaaake!"

"Say my name again... just like that," he whispered in my ear as he gave a hard couple of thrusts and pulled out again.

"Blaaa..." my voice cracked when I was saying it again as he slowly slid back in continuing to tease me. I closed my eyes and it felt like I left my body for a moment. Blake's moans became more intense as he joined me in a blissful state.

Still in the same position, my eyes began to look like newly formed puddles from a sudden storm. He looked at me worriedly and said, "Baby, what is it?"

"Is this what you came over here for, Blake?"

His expression was of amazement that I would say or ask him such a thing. "Absolutely not! I came over here because I wanted... I want to be with you and only you."

"I don't believe you, Blake. I don't believe you. Get up!"

He quickly sat up and I saw his eyes start to well up. "Baby, why... why would you think that? I'm not these other dudes you've dealt with. I'm Blake... I..."

I interrupted him and said, "Exactly, you... are... Blake."

"Oh, my goodness, Nefertiti?! Baby! Please..."

Interrupting him again, I said, "You got what you wanted. So, you can leave now. Just get out!"

His tears started to fall. "Baby, wait a minute... please... please don't..."

"Leave! Get out, Blake!" I yelled at him again with the utmost intent of hurting him, too. He knew I meant what I said by my tone. So, he gathered his clothes and started walking towards the door.

He stopped to put them on and said, "Baby, that's not what I came over here for. I know that I hurt you and you are probably doing this to get back at me and I understand... but I'm not giving up. We will be together. It might not be tonight... but it will be soon. I believe that with everything that I am. You are the one I'm supposed to be with. You are the one that I have always longed for. I'm... I'm not going to give up on us, because I know you feel the same way about me as I do about you. If I'm wrong, then tell me that now."

I didn't say a word because he was right. Blake walked out of the door, and I sat there sobbing uncontrollably. I was definitely more in love with him than I wanted to admit. My emotions became so overwhelming as I slid down off the couch sitting on the floor.

I buried my head in the couch pillow that had fallen earlier, and it soaked up my tears. Still distraught, I cried myself to sleep. About an hour later, I awoke realizing that I was still in the same position completely naked. I slowly walked into my bedroom and looked in the mirror. I saw that my eyes were so red and puffy from crying.

Zyaire called and texted earlier to see if I was ok, but, of course, I was 'preoccupied.' I just now texted him back that I was alright, completely lying. He wanted to come back; but in my response, I told him not to do so.

I showered and got in the bed. It took me so long to go to sleep. Blake had called and texted several times, but I didn't answer or respond to him. I finally drifted off about an hour and

a half later again crying myself to
sleep.

The next morning, I woke up to
more missed calls and texts from Blake.
He had attempted to get in contact with
me throughout the night and most of the
early morning. I never responded to
him, not even when I saw them when I
woke up. There was another from Zyaire,
but I didn't respond to him either
until the following day asking if we
could talk.

A couple days after that night,
Zyaire came over to discuss our
'situation'. The first thing out of his
mouth was, "First, of all, I didn't
know you dealt with celebrities."

"Zyaire, he... it's a long story."

"I've got time. I'll always have
time for you... always."

I smiled.

"There it is. That's what I wanted
to see."

"It's a whirlwind that I really
don't want to discuss right now. I
wanted to talk to you because... I
don't think we can go any further with
us other than being the friends that we
are right now. I need some time just to

myself to clear my head... just focus on what I need and want. I'm sorry if that sounds cliché', but it's the truth."

"Honestly, the way bruh came to your door, I believe you... and I don't think I need to be in the same boat that he's in at the moment. Did you put a spell on him?" Zyaire and I laughed. "Whenever it is that you decide to get back into the swing of things, let me know. Do you mind if I still call or text or whatever?"

"No, I don't mind."

"Good. Good. Well, let me get out of here. I have to meet some co-workers at this great spot not too far from here."

"Café Italiano?"

"Yes, that's it."

"Oh, you're going to love it. I go there frequently. So, much so that they know me by name. Saying that out loud is kind of embarrassing."

We both looked at each other and giggled so hard. I got up to leave and I followed him to the door. Zyaire turned around and hugged me so tight. The kind of hug that said 'this was our

*last time seeing each other for a while
or ever.' We kissed and he left.*

   "So, Naquita, that's when I called
you to tell you what happened over
those last couple of days."
   "Girl, yeah, I certainly remember
that night. I was in shock, and I know
you were still confused or whatever.
So, that's why I suggested that you
needed to take some time for yourself
and decide what or who you wanted.
However, ya'll still ran up on each
other in New Orleans at the festival.
Ya'll were obviously meant for each
other. I don't think you told me
everything that happened then either.
So, get to talking!"
   "OK! You're right. So..." I
continued.

'MUSICAL WEEKEND'

A couple months had passed since seeing Blake that night. Before breaking up, we had made plans to go to the Music Festival in New Orleans this upcoming weekend. But of course, that was definitely not going to happen now. On the Tuesday before that weekend, Naquita called me because Imani had asked if she was available.

Side Note: Imani is another friend of ours who we went to college with and is now a big-time reporter for a top newspaper and news station.

Apparently, Imani's two friends that were supposed to go had backed out. Naquita told Imani that she would call me to see if I was able to go.

"Hey Girl! What are you doing this weekend? I hope you don't have any plans!"

"Uhm, no, I don't, not anymore. Why do you ask? What are you up to?!"

"I'm not up to anything... this time! Imani called and said that she has two-three day passes available for the Music Festival in New Orleans this

weekend. *I told her that I would call you to see if you were up to doing something."*

"Well, I don't have anything planned now and I love New Orleans. So, hell... sure, why not?!"

"Yessss!" screamed Naquita. "This weekend is going to be epic! The three of us haven't done anything like this in a hot minute. It's supposed to be a beautiful weekend, too!"

"You're so right!" I yelled.

"Make sure you bring your bathing suit!" Naquita yelled back excitedly.

"I will! Girl, I am not looking for ANYTHING. I am just going to go so that we can hang out like we used to and have some fun," I said with a sense of determination.

"I know that you were supposed to go with Blake, but don't worry about him. It was his loss, not yours!"

"Sure was!"

"Speaking of Blake, has he tried to contact you, lately?" asked Naquita.

"No, it's been about three weeks or so. However, I have talked to his sister quite a few times. Well, darn, I talked her up. She's calling me now."

"Ok, Nef, call me later so that we can schedule flights and such. Oh yeah, she said that the rooms were already booked. You know she's a reporter. So, all of it was paid for through the company."

"Oh, shit?! For real?! Ok then! I'll call you a little later. Bye girl," I said slyly rushing her off the phone to answer Deadra's call.

"Bye!"

However, I wasn't able to switch over to Deadra in time. So, I had to call her back. "Hi D! How are you?"

"Great, sis! I was just calling to see if you had plans this weekend; that's all." I heard the sneakiness in her voice, but I ignored it.

"Yes, I do. I actually just got off the phone with Naquita. We and another friend will be in New Orleans for the Music Festival. It's always off-the-chain when us three get together!"

Blake was actually on the other end listening, but I didn't know that at the time. "Do you know what hotel ya'll are staying in?"

"No, not yet. I am supposed to call her later. We'll probably have a three-way with Imani to get ALLLLL of the details."

"Ok, sounds good. I was thinking about going and wanted to go as a girl's trip. So, since you are already going, I'll see you there sometime during the weekend, right?" asked Deadra.

"Oh, yes, of course!"

"Great! Don't forget to send me the details."

"Ok, I won't. Talk to you later."

"Bye Sis!"

As soon as I hung up, Blake and Deadra continued to talk. "Thank you, D! I miss her so much."

"I know you do. She misses you, too. She was just hurt by the whole situation, you know..."

"Yeah, I know. Believe me," Blake said sadly.

"Ok, so, as soon as I get more information, I'll let you know. Love you, B."

"Love you, too, D."

Later that night, we (Naquita, Imani and I) had a three-way convo about the details of our upcoming trip. We were beyond excited! All three of us were to arrive on Thursday but at different times. Imani who lived in Dallas would be there before us, of course. The three-day passes were for all of the happenings going on that weekend so we could come and go as we pleased. V-I-P, baby!

After talking with them, I texted the details of my flight and hotel to Deadra. She immediately sent them to Blake. Again, of course, I didn't know this at the time.

The next couple of days seemed so long because of the anticipation of all the fun to be had. I was only going to work half a day that following Thursday since my flight was supposed to leave at 2:15pm.

Finally, the day had come! I did wonder if I would see Blake, especially since his sister was going; but I quickly stopped those thoughts. I missed him in more ways than I believed I ever could, but it was what it was. We weren't together.

My flight landed at 5:55pm. Naquita had already arrived and was with Imani when she picked me up. The joy in our hearts seeing each other was unreal. We chatted and laughed the whole way back to the hotel. The only thing on our agenda for the night was getting some good food and a drink or two. Each of us had a separate room but they were all joined which was perfect. I took a shower and changed clothes. Then we headed to the gumbo restaurant around the corner.

We had so much to catch up on that we stayed at the restaurant until they closed. On our way back we stopped to listen to a band that was playing on the sidewalk. There were several other people there, as well. Most of them were dancing or rocking to the song. Naquita whispered to me, "Look over there."

She was telling me to look to my right farther down the street near the hotel entrance. She kept looking and squinting to make sure she was seeing who she thought she was. "Oh my, is that?"

When I finally looked, I yelled in a whisper, "Oh no, it's Blake! Oh, my goodness." The temperature in my entire body increased so fast that I almost fainted. He had spotted me already, but I didn't know it right then.

"Girl, you ok?" Imani asked.

"I, uh, I just need to go back to the room and lie down. It's been a long day, and I had a drink," I said with a laugh.

Naquita said, "Oh yeah, you are not the drinker in our group!"

We all laughed so hard and headed to our rooms. As soon as I got back to the room, I laid down. I checked my phone and saw that Deadra had texted me. I responded by letting her know that I had made it. She was in the same hotel and apparently so was Blake.

The next morning, I was up before anyone else and decided to get breakfast with Deadra. We met at a little spot right next to the Gumbo place. The food reminded me of this spot back home in Tennessee. Our conversation was going well until she asked me if I had talked to Blake. She confirmed that he was here, also.

"I saw him last night from a distance."

Deadre said, "Yeah, he told me that he saw you but didn't say anything."

"What's crazy is that... wait a minute. Now that I think about it... Wow?! That was him."

"What do you mean?!"

"Someone brushed up against me as he was passing by with his friends. At the time, I thought I smelled the cologne that he knows I love but kept telling myself that I didn't. Wow! Not too long after that, Naquita pointed him out in front of the hotel. That explains why the 'brush' up against me felt so familiar!"

Deadre smiled and said, "As I told you the other day, Blake really misses you. He knows he made a mistake by getting in the car with Aasira that day."

Just as Deadra said this, my phone rung. It was Naquita seeing if I was back, yet. "Oh shit, go ahead Sis. I'll catch up with you later. It was sooo good seeing you."

We walked out of the restaurant. Her friends were there waiting for her. We hugged and said our goodbyes. I looked down the street and saw that Naquita and Imani were coming my way. They had grabbed a quick bite at the hotel. We decided to go to an actors' workshop that had several speakers to discuss their trials, tribulations and inspirations. This also included the panelists sharing some advice that they received to keep them motivated in tough times.

The discussion lasted for almost an hour and a half. About an hour in, there was a surprise guest, Blake Lovingly. He stayed on the stage for about 30 minutes. Since Imani was a reporter, we had some great seats on the third row directly in front of the panelists. When Blake came out, the crowd was beyond excited to see him. I had never heard so many screams in my life. I grabbed Naquita's hand and squeezed it so tight. She already knew what I was thinking. At the very end, they asked him one question that had nothing to do with the topic.

"So, Blake, we know this last question has zero to do with what we've talked about today. But you've gotta let the ladies know if you are taken?!" the host asked with the utmost intent and curiosity.

Blake smiled and laughed so widely and said, "Well, to be perfectly honest, NO, I am not taken." The crowd went crazy again.

I had no reaction, of course. Then Blake looks right at me. I looked like a deer caught in headlights because I didn't think he knew I was there. He then continues by saying, "However, there is someone that I am extremely, extremely fond of and she knows who she is."

The host continued to pry, "Do we know her?! Is she a celebrity?!"

Still smiling, Blake said, "That's all that I'm going to say about it."

"Awww, so, you are just going to leave us hanging like that?!"

"Sorry," Blake said as he shrugged his shoulders and threw up his hands as if to continue to say, 'that's it.'

Since she didn't get any more info out of him, the host ended the panel discussion on that note. The crowd was very engaged and asked some wonderful questions the entire time. Blake and the other panelists waved to the crowd, and everyone started to exit the auditorium.

All three of us left with little gems to use and pass along. Imani got some great footage and pics to use for her job. We then decided to go back to the hotel for a moment to freshen up.

As we were heading back, I received a text from Blake, 'Hi Nefertiti. Please don't delete this. I saw that you were in the crowd and wanted to make sure that you knew my answer to that last question was directed towards you. I miss you so much. Will you please talk to me?'

Naquita and Imani saw my facial expression while I was looking at my phone. Simultaneously, both of them asked, "Is that from Blake, Nef?"

"Yes, yes, it is."

"Are you gonna talk to this man? You need to! Shit!" both of them chimed in at the same time.

"Ok. Ok. I will talk to him. I just texted him back that I would."

"Gooooood!" yelled Naquita. "When are ya'll gonna talk? If you ain't trying to give him none, you might want to do it in a place where ya'll are not alone. You told me how ya'll are when around each other."

"It will be at the poetry club tonight."

"Perfect! Are you going to do anything?" asked Imani.

"I wasn't planning on it."

"Now, you know if they find out that you're there what's going to happen!"

"We'll see," I said with a 'I know' look.

Naquita and I stayed in our rooms for a couple hours while Imani went to the festivities. Technically, she was working; so, it was ok. I was still a little tired from the night before and so was Naquita.

I woke up around 5 feeling completely refreshed. I saw that Naquita had just got up herself. She had sent me the usual 'Get yo' ass up!' text. Since our rooms are joined, I knocked on her door to let me in.

"Girl, that was the best sleep!"

"It sure was. I needed that!" I exclaimed.

"So, are you ready to see your man!"

I looked at her, rolled my eyes and said, "Whatever!"

"You know you are. Let's be honest."

"Ok! Yes, I am. So, I am about to get all cute right now. But afterwards, I have got to get something to eat."

"You ain't said nothing but a word. I am starving, too."

I went back to my room to take a shower and change clothes. There was another text from Blake...'I can't wait to see you tonight. Like, I said earlier, I miss you.'

I sent a reply that said, 'To be honest, I miss you, too.'

He sent back three heart emojis.

After getting ready, Naquita and I were talking in my room waiting on Imani. She had come back to the room to shower and change clothes. I put on a white crop top, light-colored, split detail jeans and clear, heeled, mule sandals. My hair was in its naturally, curly state... voluptuous, as always.

It was now 6:36pm and we were all finally ready to go and get something to eat. Afterwards, we were going to partake in a little poetry at a very popular spot about 9 minutes from the hotel.

We decided to again go to the gumbo spot around the corner. It was sooo good the other day that we just had to circle back.

It was now 7:02pm and we finally got our food. The place was really busy which was actually not a surprise. The food and atmosphere were again phenomenal.

"So, Nef, you ready to see your man?!" asked Imani knowing that Naquita had asked me that earlier.

"He is not my man! Thank you very much!"

They both laughed, "Yeah right! If you say so...!"

Naquita added, "Now you know that's not what you said a couple hours ago!"

Laughing hysterically, we continued to talk and eat. I didn't drink anything this time. However, Imani and Naquita did, of course. The poetry spot was about a 6 minute walk from the restaurant. This gave us an opportunity to try to avoid the I-TIS by 'walking the food' down some.

During our walk, we saw some great vendors. One had a plethora of unique jewelry; thus, each of us had to buy a piece. By the time we made it to the club, it was 8:12pm when I looked at my watch. We paid our entry fee and walked in. Naquita saw that there was a second level which was perfect. We headed up there to grab a table. The place reminded me of the one in Philadelphia. You were able to see the stage from any angle. It was quite big but cozy at the same time. The ambiance was amazing.

As soon as we sat down, they started with the performers. We had perfect timing. Naquita leaned over and said, "Hey Nef, I don't see Blake, yet. Do you?"

"I wasn't looking. Let me see." Both of them gave me a side-eye because they knew I was lying. Just as my eyes turned towards the door, they got wide with surprise and anticipation.

"Uh oh, I know that look! He's here, isn't he?" Naquita said excitedly.

"Yes, he - he just walked in." They couldn't tell it was him, but I would know him anywhere. It didn't matter how much he tried to hide or be disguised. He had on a hat turned backwards and shades with a relaxed white tee and relaxed jeans that still hugged every part of him in the right places. He was with Deuce and Tre', his boys since forever. Neither of them were in a relationship. So, there was no telling what they were about to or have already gotten into this weekend.

"Hey B, you supposed to see yo' girl tonight, right?" asked Deuce teasingly.

"Yeah, she's already here up top."

They headed to the second floor to find us. Blake spotted me and I saw him heading our way. I couldn't see his eyes, but I felt them. "Look who's getting nervous!" Imani teased and shouted.

"I AM NOT!" I responded knowing damn well that I really was.

Blake said, "Hi Nef." He held out his hands for me to give him a hug. Our embrace was full-bodied and lovingly tight (no pun intended) that lasted for a little more than a moment. Everyone hugged and got introduced to each other. Of course, I already knew Deuce and Tre'.

"So, what are ya'll getting into after this?" asked Blake.

"We were actually going to stay here, because I heard it turns into a club-like atmosphere after the poetry set," I answered.

"Sounds cool. We might check it out for a moment."

Blake still had on his sunglasses. He pulled my chair closer to him so that we could have a little bit of privacy. He whispered in my ear, "Baby, I miss you. Can we just..."

Before he could finish his sentence, the host got on stage and said, "Whassup, ya'll?! I hope ya'll are having a good time tonight!" The crowd cheered as he continued. "Guess who I was told was in the build-ing to-night?"

"Who?!" yelled the crowd.

"One of our favorites, Nefertiti!"

The crowd cheered even louder. "I know she's not on the list tonight, but I was hoping that she would bless us with a little something."

They shined the light on me. I was not prepared to be on stage.

The host said, "I know that you may not be prepared, but you had to know that if we found out that you were here that we'd ask you to come to the stage and do something for us."

The crowd continued with a persuasive cheer to get me to get on stage. When I got up, it was the biggest roar I had ever heard. Deuce and Tre' looked at Blake who had a smile on his face.

When I walked on stage, the host said, "Since you weren't prepared, can I make a request?"

I nodded 'yes'.

"Yessss! Will you please do 'Knock'? It's one of my favorites because of your delivery!"

"Yes, I will!" With a wide grin on his face, he handed me the mic. I then started saying the poem.

I could see that Blake still had a huge smile on his face. Deuce leaned over to Blake and asked, "Hey man, wasn't this the poem she did in Philadelphia when you first saw her?"

"Yeah, it is," Blake said while reminiscing.

"Damn, how ironic!" proclaimed Deuce.

When I finished, I thanked everyone. Then the host came back on stage. He said, "Now that's what I'm talking about. It didn't even matter that she wasn't on the list. She still came with that fire! Yessss! Thank you, Nefertiti! Oh, yeah, ya'll get her book! It's available everywhere!"

As I headed back to my seat, several people gave me compliments. Blake was the first one to greet me at our table to hug me again. "Baby, that was absolutely awesome, as usual!"

"Thank you, Blake."

His tone changed when he said, "Now, can we finish our conversation." He removed his sunglasses and looked me straight in my eyes seductively. The moment I saw that, I lowly uttered, 'uhmmm' as I closed my eyes and quickly looked away.

"I see that even now when I look at you, it still has the same affect, huh," he said as he grabbed my hand and lightly kissed it. His lips were still soft like I remembered. I again looked away.

Blake grabbed my face and turned my head around so that we could look each other in the eyes again. "Nef, baby, tell me what I need to do."

"It's not that simple, Blake."

"I know, baby. Just tell me something that I can do to start."

"We can just... just work on our friendship again."

"Friends?!" he said surprisingly.

I nodded.

"Ok. Friends it is, but the way you just reacted when I looked at you like... this," Blake said while lowering his voice and giving me that look again. "How is that going to work?"

"Oooohhh weeee," I muttered under my breath trying to hide my feelings at that very moment. "It will. It will."

"Alright, alright," he said as he slowly let my hand go.

"Uhm, excuse me for a second. I am gonna go to the restroom. I'll be right back." I had to go regroup. Oh, my goodness, this man!

While I was in the bathroom, I received a text from Blake saying that he and his boys were headed to another spot. He also wanted to come by my room later if I was up. I didn't tell him 'yes' but I certainly didn't tell him 'no' either. I missed him so much.

Imani, Naquita and I stayed at the poetry spot turned club for another couple hours. Then we headed back to the hotel since we had a lot of things planned for the next day. On the way back, Naquita asked me about Blake.

"So, are ya'll back together?! We saw the interaction between ya'll and it looked very intense."

"No, we are not. We are going to try to be friends first. However, I'm not gonna lie. He still makes my entire being glow with even just the slightest smile, look or touch... Shit!"

"Yeah, we saw that. So, are you gonna give him some or what?"

"Look now! No, I am not."

"Not even if he comes to your room tonight?! Yeah right! We'll make sure to have our earbuds in to not hear ya'll! Ewwww!" said Naquita as she and Imani burst out laughing. All I could do was laugh, too.

When we got back to the hotel, we talked for a little bit more in Naquita's room. After finishing our cackling, we decided to turn in for the night. Just as I was walking into my room, I saw my phone light up. It was Blake. He and his friends had just come back to the hotel. He texted that he was going to take a shower and come to my room if that was ok with me. I hesitantly replied to him that it was.

I sat on the bed for a moment thinking about our first encounter and how just seeing him still made me feel that way. After about six minutes, I got in the shower. As soon as I was about to get out, there was a knock on the door. "Baby, it's me."

"Ok, one moment!" I said as I was stepping out wrapping the towel around me. So, this meant that I was still wet because I didn't have a chance to dry

off. I slipped on my flip flops and rushed to the door.

When I opened it for him to come in, I made sure that I was standing behind the door. He walked in wearing jogging pants (he knew exactly what he was doing) and a muscle shirt.

Blake quickly realized that I was in a towel and still wet and said, "Damn, baby, still beautiful and as sexy as ever."

That of course made me smile.

I tried not to let it show and said, "Blake, what else did you want to talk about?"

Blake came towards me slowly walking me back up against the wall. He looked at me like he did earlier and began kissing me deeply and then said, "Nefertiti, I want you. I still don't want to be anywhere else but here with you."

That was all he had to say, and I gave in easily. While we continued to kiss, I reached down into his jogging pants and quickly confirmed that he didn't have on any underwear. I wanted to make sure that 'he' was ready (although I could already see it), and 'he' definitely was.

"Blake, do you have...?"

Smiling, he said, "Yes, baby, right here." He said this while pulling out the condom and slipping it on.

Still hugged up on the wall, he slowly removed my towel admiring every inch of me. While firmly gripping my thighs, he lifted me and held me up against the wall. As he was sliding in, we both let out the most satisfying moan. About six minutes in, the fire alarm went off which meant we had to stop and evacuate the building.

"Blake, we..."

"I know! Damn! Please don't tell me to stop right now," he replied with no interruption whatsoever in his thrusts.

"Blaaaake..."

"Yeeeesss, baby."

"We... oh my... we need to..." I stopped trying to talk as the buildup of the tension between us became more intense and pleasingly left our bodies. It was like our souls jumped out of us and danced.

Even though the alarm was still going off, we stared at each other for a moment in awe of what just happened. Unfortunately, there was no time for a shower. So, a quick wash had to do for the moment. As I was putting on some clothes, he went to the bathroom to remove the condom and do the same. He put his sunglasses and hat back on. Then we walked out of the room.

As soon as we walked out, I saw Naquita and Imani who had the biggest smiles on their faces. Naquita mouthed to me, "I knew it! I knew it!"

I couldn't do anything but shake my head and so did Blake. Thankfully, the fire alarm incident only lasted for fifteen minutes. Everyone hurried back inside. Naquita and Imani were staring at us and smiling. Blake lowkey followed me back to my room.

When we walked in, Blake said, "Nef, I don't want to be just your friend. My love for you goes waaaay beyond that."

"Blake..."

Just as I was about to respond, his phone started going off with text after text after text. He said, "Baby, one moment... What the fuck?!"

As he was reading his texts, I could tell that he was furious and hurt. "This is some straight bullshit! Baby, I gotta go. I'm sorry. I'll explain later. Just please, please be patient with me. I love you... ok."

Blake kissed me and walked out.

"But wait..." Naquita said. "Ya'll didn't see each other anymore that weekend, did you?"

"No, but we were supposed to. However, his ex, Aasira, had posted on her page that she was pregnant, and that Blake was the father."

"Oh, damn, girl! That heifer is something else."

"Yes, she is. He, of course, wanted to make sure before making any rash decisions, not that it would affect his love for me. So, he needed to talk to her."

Blake went to see Aasira to talk about the baby. She avoided going to the doctor for a couple weeks. During that time, she tried to sleep with him on several occasions but that didn't work; nothing happened. Blake knew something seemed off about the whole situation. The timeline just wasn't adding up. He was finally able to get her to go to the doctor for an ultrasound. It turned out that the broad wasn't even pregnant. She had used a test from a friend of hers who was pregnant to try and trick Blake."

"How did you find out about this?"

"He told me."

"How is that when ya'll haven't talked. Well, since I didn't answer his calls. He left all this in voicemails and texts. You would think that it would deter him, but as you can see, it hasn't. I mean he's here in New York."

"Exactly! Now that's some deep love right there, man. Damn! Ya'll put a spell on each other like a muthafucka!"

THE KNOCK

Naquita and I were still talking when I looked at my watch. It was 2:22pm. Blake was supposed to be here in the next few minutes. I stopped talking suddenly.

"Dang, girl, what's wrong with you?!" She realized that I just looked at my watch. "Ohhhh, I see. It's almost that time, ain't it?!"

"Shut up!"

"You look so nervous!"

"I am... I really am."

"Just listen to what he has to say. Now, whether you believe him or not, that's up to you but both of ya'll need closure on this... whichever direction it is."

Agreeing with Naquita, I said, "You're right."

"I know you love him. So, just don't be scared to be open with him about your feelings and what you want. That's all I'm saying."

I nodded in agreement. Then we heard a knock on the door. Blake arrived with one minute to spare. I looked at Naquita and she looked at me whispering, "Girl, open the door."

I opened the door and Blake was there smiling, "Hi." He said it like I took his breath away when he saw me.

"Hi," I said mimicking his tone unintentionally but admiring how sexy he looked. All he had on was a loose hunter green tee, khakis and white/khaki/hunter green sneakers, but with him it doesn't even matter.

"Well, I guess, I'll let you two lovebirds... I mean... I guess I'll leave you two alone so ya'll can talk." Naquita hugged me as she walked out. "I'm watching you, Blake."

He threw up his hands and gave an 'I didn't do anything' look while saying, "Yes, ma'am."

When I closed the door, I then turned around. Blake was standing right there. He didn't say a word. He just pulled me close and tightly hugged me in such a way that I should have lost my breath. Instead, I inhaled and exhaled slowly reveling in the moment of being back in his arms.

Coming back to my senses, I quickly snapped out of it and pushed him away. Blake said, "Baby, please don't push me away."

"You said you wanted to talk... so talk, Blake."

"Nefertiti, I... I missed you more than words could ever express. I apologize wholeheartedly for hurting you and all of the misunderstandings. I never... never meant to do that. I love you. I've always loved you. There is no comparison to what we had... to what we have. I..."

"Blake, don't..."

He slowly came closer as I saw his eyes tearing up. His eyes were like a vast ocean that I always found myself drowning in from the very first moment that I saw him. "Baby, please... please give me another chance. Please."

He gently grabbed my waist to pull me close to him again. The tears I had been holding back since he started talking began to roll my down face.

"Blake..."

As soon I said his name, I was in complete boo-hoo mode which made his eyes become a waterfall, as well. It seemed like we were both allowing ourselves to let go... exhale the pain, the misunderstandings... the 'stank

air' and inhale new beginnings, fresh
air. But...

"Blake... I-I need to leave for a
moment."

"Ok, I'll..."

"No, I need to go by myself."

"Al-alright," he said as he wiped
his tears. "Baby, just come back to me
and say you'll give me the chance to
prove it to you in every way possible,"
he said as he wiped my tears and
caressed my cheek.

When I turned around and walked
out of the room closing the door behind
me, I leaned up against it. It seemed
like I could feel him doing the same
thing. That's how strong our connection
had always been. I stayed there for
about a minute and walked away.

When I got to the lobby, I sat in
the farthest corner that I could away
from other people. I didn't want anyone
to see me crying. However, a few of the
hotel personnel saw me anyway and asked
if I was ok. I was gone for about 20
minutes.

My thoughts were only of us. I was
going back and forth wondering if
giving Blake another chance was a

mistake or was it just me being scared to take that chance. He was EVERYTHING I had ever wanted in a man, The Perfect Fit. Not because of WHO he was, because I didn't care about that, and he knew it. But it was because I could actually be ME with him... be FREE with him... feel PROTECTED by him... feel LOVED by him... be ENCOURAGED by him. His aura from day one had always been on another level that I was easily drawn to. Blake made LOVE... LIFE seem easy just being around him.

At that moment, I said to myself, 'Nef, get your butt upstairs and claim your man!' I jumped up and hurriedly headed toward the elevator. When I got there, I pressed the button to call it to come to the lobby.

As I was waiting nervously, my phone buzzed. It was Naquita texting, "Are ya'll back together, yet? Ya'll better be!" I just shook my head. By that time, the elevator doors opened, and I went in pressing the 6 button for my floor.

I then texted her that I would talk to her later. She responded with 'Alright, make sure you do.'

When the doors opened for me to exit, I hesitated and took a deep breath; then walked out. Once I got to the door of my room, I realized that I had left my key. So, I hoped that Blake would still be there. However, if he's not, then I knew that my previous thoughts were for nothing; and my feelings were to be flushed out for good this time.

As I lightly knocked, I could hear footsteps coming towards the door. 'He's still here,' I thought to myself feeling relieved. Blake opened it and I saw that his eyes were still red as if he had just finished sobbing again.

"Nefertiti, you're back!" he said like a frog had magically appeared in his throat while moving out of the way to let me in.

"Hi, Blake. I - I love you. I'm in love with you, too." I paused for a moment and sat on the bed looking over at him. "I always have been. Yes, I... I want to be with you. I'll give you another chance."

"That's all I need, baby. That's all I need. I haven't been with anyone else but you since you kicked me out that day. I just couldn't and I didn't want anyone else," Blake whispered as I could see tears form in his eyes again while coming towards me. He knelt in front of me looking in my eyes with the most loving look that I had ever seen from any man. Blake grabbed my face, leaned in and kissed me.

It had been over four months since we last kissed. Melting at this moment was an understatement. It became more passionate as our tongues did dances that only Africa could choreograph. As he leaned me to scoot me back on the bed, his phone rang. It was his management team, but, of course, he didn't want to answer. Then Blake proceeded to remove his shirt.

"Not now, guys." It rang again. "Shit! One moment, baby, one moment."

Blake stood up and grabbed his phone. All I could do was stare at the specimen standing in front of me. His shoulders were so broad and defined just like I remember. He was working out again for an upcoming movie and it definitely showed.

Then he turned around, 'Hmmm.'

Blake heard me and turned back around seeing me bite my lip while looking at him. He raised his eyebrow and gave me a little, devilish grin. Then he motioned for me to remove my clothes.

Blake was still on the phone as he watched me slowly remove my shirt... my jeans. He gestured for me to stop when I was about to remove my bra and panties. He mouthed, "Keep those on." I winked at him and did a little devilish grin of my own.

He finally got off the phone and said, "Guess what, Nef?!"

"What?!"

"You are looking at the new owner of a huge space for my production company here in New York!"

"What!? Seriously?! Wow?! Congratulations, Blake!"

"Yes, thank you. I am super excited! This is an epic move! Now, come here," he said as he removed his khakis and boxer briefs crawling back on the bed.

He pulled my hips towards him teasing me as he likes to do. Removing my bra, he started kissing every inch of me with each movement down towards my stomach... my pelvis. Opening my legs even further, he continued with my thighs... inner thighs pulling my panties to the side, he proceeded to kiss, devour my velvet center.

In only five minutes, I was merely a puddle of chocolate that he was about to dip his pretzel in... double dip that is. This time was different. We made love... not that we never had but this was beyond what we had experienced before.

Blake's strokes were unhurried and intentional in every way possible that seemed to take away any leftover pent up fears that either of us had. 'He' filled the emptiness that plagued 'her.' 'She' swallowed every single inch. 'He' filled the void that lingered. 'She' was able to let go of all the pain, the sadness, the lost love. Our souls were finally complete. Both of us had the sweetest release.

He stayed on top of me for a moment (as he likes to do). However, I think this time was more so because even the aftershocks were intense. He then raised his head looking at me with

those hypnotizing eyes. "What's wrong?"
He asked because he saw my eyes well up
and the tears slowly began to fall as
he looked at me.

"Nothing. Nothing's wrong. I
just... I..." I couldn't say what I was
thinking as I was overcome with emotion
as the tears kept falling.

"You don't have to say anything
else," Blake says as he wiped my tears
and kissed me all over my face. I felt
him growing inside of me again.

"Blllaaaaaake!" I whispered.

"That's it, Nefertiti. I'm here
now and I'm not going anywhere." We
both were about to reach our peak
again, but I decided that I wanted to
be in charge this time. So, I whispered
in his ear for him to let me. I was his
jockey taking the reins controlling his
every jolt. Blake tried to grab me to
pause for a moment, but I didn't let
him. I grabbed his hands and pinned
them above his head.

"Ba-by... wait... hold-," he
couldn't finish his sentence as he
closed his eyes.

I knew that, in actuality, he
could have overpowered me if he really

wanted to, but he didn't. Blake tried
to speak again, but I kissed him so
that he couldn't. A few moments later,
he broke free of my grasp pulling and
holding me close to him with one hand.
With the other, he gripped my cheeks to
hold me in place while he took over. We
kept riding the wave until we both hit
the shore. How was it possible that
this time was on an even higher level
of ecstasy for the both of us?!

Blake wrapped his arms around
me... holding me as he lightly caressed
my back. We laid there enjoying the
closeness as the sweat poured from our
bodies. In a low, deep tone, he said,
"Nef, I love you. Again... baby, I'm in
love with you. I always have been. Like
I said the very first time, I'm not
going anywhere. Baby, you're stuck with
me." This was a feeling that I had
always longed for.

After showering, we both fell fast
asleep. I was in my rightful place, his
arms as the little spoon. A few hours
had passed, and I suddenly woke up
because I had to use the bathroom. I
laid back in the bed staring at him.
His back was towards me, and I was

admiring his tattoos. One of them I didn't remember seeing, a small heart with my initials that looked quite fresh. Of course, my eyes filled with tears again, and I got back up. Overcome with emotion, I pulled out my pin and paper and began to write...

It is not supposed to hurt like hell
But only cast a spell
Over my mind, body, and soul
Making me feel warm not cold
But making my heart skip a beat
With each touch that he makes
When he takes me
On a roller coaster ride
Flying high in the clouds
Moving in slow motion
Like the gentle wave of an ocean
As a breeze
Sends sensuous smells
That overwhelms
My sense of self
Hypnotizing
Tantalizing
My breath
As I hold it

Never wanting to let it go
As the blood through me flows
To each and every limb
With just the smallest thought of him
And even when he is not around
I can still hear his voice
Its enchanting sound
Making him my only choice
As I glow
Like a candle enflamed
Because he
Plays no games
Because he is like
That king-size candy bar that satisfies whenever I crave
Because he
Quenches my thirst
Like cold water on a hot, summer day
That captivates
Titillates
And percolates
As I explode inside
Like dynamite
As every millimeter of my being is satisfied
Because that's what
IT IS
supposed to be like

THE
PERFECT FIT

It was 9:02pm when we heard running through the hallway. We awoke still in each other's arms. He caressed my back and tickled my ear to wake me up. Blake said, "Damn, did you hear that?"

Still trying to fully awake, I said, "Yes, I did."

"It's just 9:06. I don't know about you but uhhhh I'm starving."

"I am, too, actually," I said feeling equally famished.

"Good! Do you want to order room service, or do you want to go grab a bite somewhere?" asked Blake.

"Room service is fine."

"Cool, I'll send it up to my room. Uhm, baby?"

"Yes, Blake."

"How about you cancel your room and come stay with me? You were going to leave on the same day I was anyway. I don't want to be without you... don't want to be away from you anymore, plus we can be as loud as we want to." He said that last statement with a wink.

With no hesitation, I said, "Ok, I will. I don't either. Let me call the front desk and talk to them about it."

"Actually, wait... I'll have my assistant call and do it. They'll probably call you to verify."

Blake proceeds to call his assistant as I gather my things to go to his room. Sure enough, about ten minutes later, the front desk called to verify the information that they received. They told me that they would refund my entire stay.

"The power of you, huh?!"

"I know when to use it and when not to, baby," Blake said as he playfully slapped me on my butt. "You ready? Room service will be there in about 10 more minutes."

"Yes, I'm ready." We went up to his room on the fifteenth floor. It looked like an apartment. "Oh, wow, Blake."

"Yeah, it's really nice. When I first got here, I was like 'I see why she chose this hotel.'" He pulled off his clothes, only leaving on his boxer briefs and just put on a robe.

"Blake, what if - what would have happened if I didn't say that I wanted to try again?"

We sat on the bed and continued talking. "Honestly, Nef, I-I don't know. However, I do know that I would have literally broken down since I love you as much as I do. I realized a while back that I've loved you since I first saw you in Philadelphia. You are like no one I have ever met... no one."

He leaned over, kissed me and said, "I would have fought for you. I would have kept trying. If I didn't think you felt the same, I would have let you go. I wouldn't have come here, but I knew you did. I know you do. I bet you are wondering how I knew you were coming to New York, huh? I still talk to your mother and my sister still talks to you, too. Well, I also have Naquita's number that I got from your mom."

"Oh really... I need to talk to the all of them about that."

"Nefertiti, my heart ached for you. My soul was empty without you. I couldn't breathe without you. I missed you so much."

I was speechless. We gazed into each other's eyes and was interrupted by room service knocking on the door.

We laughed a little because the sudden sound startled us even though we knew they were coming.

Luckily for him and me too, today was his cheat day. We ordered burgers, fries and onion rings... a plethora of items we really didn't need but we were starving. After Blake finished eating (he always finishes before me), he sat at the table for a moment because he was full. Then he went over to the window.

"You know, this is the first time that I really looked out of this window to see the view of the city. The moon is full and so bright. It's absolutely beautiful. Another reason that I came (although you're the main reason but it just happened to work out this way), was the spot for my production company. Attached to the property is space to create a really nice condo. It has over 4,000 square feet. So, I can build several bedrooms, bathrooms and sooo much more into it. It is definitely an architectural staple. I am supposed to go back and sign the paperwork tomorrow plus get the keys. Will you go with me?"

I had finished eating and was just sitting at the table not only because I was full but admiring him. He is absolutely heaven sent. "Yes, I will go with you," I say as I get up to go look out the window with him.

He wrapped his arms around me from behind and said, "You can actually see the building from here. There it is... right there... over to the right."

"Wow, Blake! It is a masterpiece."

"Tell me about it!" he said as he pulled me closer and kissed me.

"So, what does this mean for us?"

"It means that I'll be spending time here and in L.A. You know that I have investments and upcoming projects here, as well."

"Yes, I know."

"Baby, please understand that I would never ask you to just stop or quit whatever you're doing. I know you have a lot of wonderful things going on that I am so proud of you for. Plus, I know you wouldn't anyway." He laughed as he saw my reflection in the window side-eyeing him. "I'm ok with that. I believe that everything is going to work out this time. I really do."

"And Blake, I would never ask you to stop anything that you were trying to do either. I completely understand the kind of mindset and drive that you have, the reasoning behind all that you do. I know I will have some lonely nights and days because of that, but I also know that you are mine and I am yours."

"Exactly!"

"I can deal with it; even though, I have seen the way women throw themselves at you."

"Baby, you don't have to worry about that."

"Blake, all I ask is that you always come home."

"Nef... look at me." Blake turned me around and looked me straight in my eyes and continued, "I... LOVE... YOU. Do you understand that?"

"Yes, Blake, but..."

"Babe, there is no *but* needed. I swear there isn't. I will always come home to you... always. As, I said, you don't have to worry about me. I've had my 'fun' or whatever; believe me."

Uttering under my breath, I said, "I'm sure you have."

He heard me and laughed as he smiled saying, "Hey now! Don't think I didn't hear that. Come here." We started laughing. Then he grabbed my hand and pulled me close to him kissing me deeply... taking my breath away with every kiss replacing it with his. Blake pulled away and headed towards his suitcase.

As he walked away, he said, "I was going to... I was going to do this Saturday if you took me back, but I think I need to do it now. I rehearsed this in so many ways. Unfortunately, I can't even remember what I was going to say exactly. So, here goes..."

Puzzled, I said hesitantly, "What-What is it, Blake?"

He turned around with something in his hand and was trying to hide it as he came towards me. "Nefertiti..."

My eyes widened as I said to myself, 'I know that's not a ring?! Is he... oh my God!' I started sobbing and he teared up, as well.

Blake grabbed my hand. He felt my balance start to buckle, "Baby, you alright?! Come sit over here." He guided me towards the couch, and we sat

down facing each other. Blake grabbed
my face gently and wiped my tears.
"Nefertiti, as I have always told you,
I love you. You are everything I have
ever wanted and needed. We finished
each other's sentences the first time
we 'met.' Where I lack, you provide.
Where I stumble, you balance me. You
put me in my place when I need it. I
know this may sound corny but babe, you
really do complete me. Being without
you was so hard for me. But the thing
that kept me going was knowing that
this very moment would come."

He got down on one knee.

"Blake..." The crocodile tears
began to fall.

"Nefertiti, will you please do me
the honor of becoming my wife?"

It took me a moment to speak
because of all of the emotions that I
was feeling. "Yes, Blake, yes!"

He let out a sigh of relief as he
slid the ring on my finger. It was a 3
carat heart-shaped black diamond on a
rose gold band. He then picked me up
twirling me around happily; then let me
down as we started to kiss.

Ready for round 3, Blake slowly removed my pajama shirt. As he made his way down my entire body, I moaned with each kiss. He slowly pulled down my pajama shorts, still kissing every inch of me. I pulled his head up to get him to stand up. I could already see that he was standing at the utmost attention.

I opened his robe kissing his chest... slowly moving towards the very essence of him. Pulling down his boxers, I exposed him and returned the favor from earlier until he was about to climax, but he stopped me.

He said as he gained back control, "Nef, baby, SHIT! Hold on. Get up and turn around."

As I followed his orders, he finished pulling off his robe and grabbed me from behind walking me over to the bed. Then he slowly bent me over. With a deep, demanding tone, he said, "Get yo' ass up there!"

I didn't hesitate and got on all fours. With barely a second passing after assuming the position, he grabbed my hips and slowly entered me. We moaned so loud.

Blake's strokes were as long and as deep as a river. He moved us up in the bed a little further to get on his knees from behind making my bottom lip quiver. There was no interruption whatsoever in his technique. I started reaching for the sheets trying to get away. Of course, he knew what was coming.

"Unh, unh, baby ... you're not going a-ny-where ..." Blake made sure I didn't escape by gently but firmly gripping my hips holding me in place as he kept hitting my spot. It was much more overwhelming than earlier as I couldn't handle it and just fell on the bed.

"Uhhh huh..." Blake said as he eased up a little bit and stopped for a moment.

'She' was pulsating, throbbing in the depths of pleasure's ocean. Pulling out, he kissed my back moving down towards my cheeks awakening every nerve ending in my body. He gave me a little bite and we both laughed.

"You ok, baby?"

"Yes."

He always asks me if I'm ok because he knows what kind of effect he has when it comes to the bedroom. Some might say it's a little cocky, but I don't think so.

"Good," he whispered opening my legs wider because I was still on my stomach.

'He' proceeded to bring the thunder with ease as 'she' was still raining inside. He started his stroke again as it was his turn now. It felt like he was taking a walk down by the beach as the sun started to set. My body no longer belonged to me; it was his and I had no problem with it whatsoever.

We repositioned to our sides as he gently grabbed my neck. I was about to have another release as my breathing switched up and so did his... we were in sync as we so often times would be. We both came at the same time, and we just laid there enjoying the moment. Neither of us felt like we were holding back anything anymore. We were FREE. It was a blissful, euphoric feeling. We were to soon be husband and wife and be happy together forever. We fell asleep in that same position.

Later that night, I woke up to take a shower. But before I did, I quietly got up and walked to the dresser. I then looked over at him as I could see him through the mirror. I smiled and blushed at the same time. This man loved me... and it felt soooo good. I started walking over towards him to wake him up to shower but immediately stopped. I found a piece of paper and a pen because my emotions became overwhelming causing me to write... THE PERFECT FIT.

It's not only what I can do for you
Nor only what you can do for me
But what we can do for each other
Because I wanna be more than just
your lover
I wanna be your best friend
So you'll never be alone
Giving you a shoulder to cry on
I wanna be the answer to your every question
The mystery that keeps you guessing
And never straying

But always coming home
I wanna be the truth you seek
Your...wife...
I wanna be the only one to love you until the end of
time...
I wanna be in your walk
Your every step
Your stride
So much so
That if anyone asks
You'll say that I'm the reason why...
I wanna be the wine in your glass
That gets better with age
The irresistible, sensuous embrace
That always lets me have my way...
I wanna be the ink in your pen
The blood in your veins
That runs deep...
I wanna be the love in your heart
The twinkle in your eyes
That's only caused by me...
I wanna be the whisper
That tickles your eardrum
Causing an erotic sensation all throughout
Making your entire body numb
To the thoughts of anyone else ever coming about...
I wanna be the rose in your garden
That blossoms all year round

The cause of jealous eyes all over town…
I wanna be the meaning
The explanation
For your very existence
Your backbone
Your soul
The missing element
That completes you
Makes you whole…

THE END
or
shall I say
THE
BEGINNING.